CARA SU MASON

A Coffee somewhere BETWEEN dangerous AND Boring

BOOK 1

ISBN 9780473762780

Cover by Cara Su Mason
Original photo of coffee cup by zoskey on Pixabay.com
Published 2025

Content Warning

Although it is a comedy, the story in *A Coffee Somewhere Between Dangerous and Boring* does deal with death and has horror elements.

Warnings for: Death of people (onscreen and offscreen), death of a pet (offscreen), attempted harm of an animal, PTSD, mention of depression, workplace abuse, violence, and the supernatural (spirits and monsters).

To anyone who's lost right now.

Contents

COFFEE

The girl on the street was dead, and the man with a cigarette in his mouth crouched over her and pressed a ceramic cup to her lips.

It was just after the early traffic that he'd found her. One moment, that spot on the sidewalk had been empty. He'd left as women in high heels and men in business loafers had swarmed the side street to get to work. When it was finally empty, and he'd returned to have his cigarette break, she was lying there, gray and dead, with black hair and a nice coat and a terrible, torn-up beanie.

A teleporting dead person. Not the first time he'd seen one.

There'd been some stupid plastic tag on her shirt's breast pocket. He didn't know what the words meant, but he'd seen the image: A dog embroidered in gold and black. Her hair was raven, and her moles were way too *special*. Emil knew then that she was the one, especially since the narration hovered over her and wouldn't seem to go away until he did something about it.

So he gave her some elevation with his jacket and pressed the coffee cup to her lips.

That pallor cleared instantly. Her eyes fluttered open, unfocused, dark brown and nearly pitch. She looked at him. She took a sharp breath in—

"Yuck," she said weakly. "My mouth tastes disgusting." Her eyes were on him, but they seemed far away.

"Yeah, well, being dead will do that to you," Emil said. Prying his jacket out from under her head and laying her back down, he went to add, "Congratulations on coming back, by the way."

"It tastes like espress—" Her dark eyes widened. "Wait. I died?"

"Yeah. Here's your uniform." He nudged the bundle of clothes her way. A navy shirt with a gold tiger's eye on the left, and navy cargo pants hemmed with red. She'd be the new barista. He wasn't really sure how she'd be the one, but the narration was insistent on it this time—

"Rewind those words back a few times!" She clambered into a sitting position and looked more ill than before. "I can't have died!"

"This again." He rolled his eyes behind his tinted sunglasses. His cigarette was out cold. "You people die a few times and you're all upset over nothing. I'm not dealing with this denial again. Yeah, you're *finita*. You're here. Let's go."

She stared at him, open-mouthed. Then her slanted brows snapped together as she frowned. "How am I back here, then?"

"I revived you."

"Are you a paramedic?"

Whatever the heck that was. "I'm a coffee shop owner."

Her mouth hung open again. "How the *heck* did you revive me from *death*, then?"

He pointed to the coffee cup atop the bench nearby. "Coffee, if that wasn't obvious enough."

"With that? How?!"

"It was magic coffee." Seeing her expression, he said in a louder voice, "I used magic coffee to bring you back. What's so stupid about that? You're *welcome*, by the way. You decided to appear in the worst spot and nearly got trampled on. You almost got double-killed. What were you thinking?"

Running her fingers through her long, tangled hair, she said, "I dunno, man. I can't believe you're asking me this." She shook her head furiously. "No way. This can't be real. Somebody's playing a prank on me. I'm still in Sutton!"

Wildly, she looked to the man. His pursed lips told her all she needed to know—this guy believed what he was saying. Which meant...

You decided to appear in the worst spot.

She got to her feet on battered sneakers. The buildings now consisted of far too many balconies than was reasonable. Foreign script that made her head spin, products she didn't even know existed displayed proudly in shop windows. No park in sight.

Shoot, he's serious.

"You're serious," she murmured.

"You don't have to repeat what you thought back to me!" the man snapped. Grabbing the cup, he said in a smoother tone, "Congratulations. You've arrived here. I brought you back for one reason—to be my barista.

"I'm opening a pop-up café. I've been on the lookout for a barista for a while. Your job starts right away. I'll show you around."

Frowning, the girl hung there for a second. Then she choked out, "You must be insane."

"You think I just go around reviving anyone? I needed a barista, and you appeared. You're employed."

"I just died! Why would I want to go to work?"

He chewed on his cigarette. "What else are you doing right now?"

"...Not, er, not much."

"Yeah, that's what I thought. Beats complaining on the sidewalk, right?"

"...Not really." She thought it through and realized, dully, that she had no money on her. If she truly was in another world...Which sounded really stupid...she was broke and alone. "Why are you so wound up about finding a barista, anyway?"

"You can make a coffee, right?"

She blinked in surprise. "I was actually on a course for it...um, yeah. But I don't really *like* coffee." Her stomach growled. She pressed a hand to it and added, "Hey. Maybe you could feed me and I could consider taking you up on your offer."

"Hey, maybe you can wear your uniform and get to work. I brought you back from the dead." Turning from her, he said, "Lunch is at twelve on the dot through to half past. If you miss it, just drink some coffee and keep awake. If a customer dies, we've got a broom in the cupboard and you can use the paper towels—"

"If a customer dies?"

"We've got a bit of an infestation."

"...So what, cockroaches are rising up and killing the customers? Why don't you just close it for a bit?"

"It's not that simple. We can't close shop. Evil runs through the café and it's imperative that we don't close. Monsters and evil spirits, stuff like that."

"Hey, don't just shrug that off!" Hastily, the girl took after him. Her battered running shoes split along the soles—great. "You just said there are monsters in the café! How can you run it? Scratch that, how do you expect me to work there? And how did they even get there?"

He shrugged. "We can't really do anything about it. Not that I've seen, anyway. When I open a new location, they just reappear. Think of them as décor. Adds character. Don't tick them off or you'll get bitten."

"Call the Ghostbusters or something! Who wants to work in a café with monsters?"

"Hey. Hey! Don't discriminate against what's in my café. So what if they bite a few people?"

Maybe her head had been hit just a little too hard. Dazed, the girl said, "Can't be any worse than getting bitten by a dog."

Emil was silent at that.

"Come on, then, Barista Girl," he said. "Let's go."

"My name is Lucy," she said. Her voice was small. Emil sucked a breath in through his teeth and wished his cigarette was still going. She sounded *wistful,* which meant...

A backstory.

"When I died...it was a totally normal day...I was in a park, and it was sunny, and Mikah was by me..."

Emil tuned her out because he was probably going to hear about it later on, too, and he'd rather not hear it twice.

"It's so mean," Lucy said a while after she'd monologued, her voice cracking as her eyes spilled tears. "Fate can't be that cruel. I was going to confess to him..."

Emil, now standing farther away from her, flicked his second cigarette out on the curb. "You'll get over it. You've got a life here, now," he said. It didn't really comfort her, all things considered.

"Right. Go me. First I get run over, and now I'm here working. Aren't you supposed to kick back after you pass? Why did I get livened up right back into labor?"

"Oh, and if the pop-up café fails, you're going to die with no way to get you back," the man said, grabbing the cup and starting to make his way towards the building situated many, many shops over. It was almost time to open, and they had something to do first.

Wheeling backwards, Lucy sputtered out, "*What?*"

"You heard me. If the shop shuts down, you die. For real this time."

"How would you know that?" she demanded, eyeing him suspiciously.

"Look, if the café goes bust, you disappear! It's in the story. I don't make the rules."

He looked pretty sure of his apparent powerlessness. Lucy wondered dully if his time here—or his coffee—had turned his wits. Surely they weren't in a story.

"Is there *anything else* I need to know?" she asked weakly.

"Nothing else," Emil said as he made for this side street's thirty-second building. He didn't bother elaborating and adding, *for now.*

CAT

In the span of their somewhat long walk along thirty-one shops this side of the street, Lucy thought of running. The only problem, she found, was that this city was a bizarre example of structural inauthenticity, and the streets were so winding in the distance that she couldn't fathom getting far. Most of the high-rises had balconies and climbing hedges stacked on top of one another. Every sign was in a foreign script, and the images on them—one being a white cat with what seemed to be eyes to its right—made no sense.

Seeing a woman on the street flick through her change, Lucy also noticed that the money was a strange cross between paper and metal. She didn't know if that woman was rich or not.

Knowing that she was broke but still hoping that she could muster a penny, Lucy rummaged through the pockets of her coat for anything that could be of use or trade to get out of Emil's grip and came up with nothing. Not even a paperclip. *Great.*

Sourly, as they stopped outside a blue-and-white-striped awning, she reflected that, for now, she really would have to listen to Emil.

Who was now folding his arms. They looked quite skinny with that red jacket slung over his left shoulder, in all honesty, for as mundanely severe as he looked.

"You finished?" he asked.

Lucy blinked at him, then decided it was better not to question him. Instead, she turned to this café full of monsters.

It...looked surprisingly clean and welcoming.

A cozy outdoor seating arrangement. Beyond that, pale brick walls. Two stories high. The windows were dark but shining. On the ground floor were large glass panels—darkened, but she could see ivy and perhaps the outline of chairs and tables—and the pavement was swept. In the height of the day, it even looked inviting.

"This is it?" she asked.

Emil, in answer, strode over to the door and flicked through his keys. Then he paused and tried the door. "Great," he muttered. "My *employees* are still here. I thought they died..."

"Isn't that a good thing that your employees are here?" Lucy asked. "Wait, what?"

A pause.

The man turned to her. "Well, you'd better get going inside."

"What?"

"After you."

Suspiciously vague. This *could* be an elaborate plan for something nefarious, she thought. A slew of horrible things could happen. She glanced back at the weird landscape. *He did revive me from the dead...And he's not in a rush to get me through the door. I doubt my chances would be better anywhere else...I guess I'll be employed for like a day. Tops.*

Taking a deep breath in, she walked past the tall man and entered the threshold.

It was dark inside. Very little sunlight warmed the interior. She could see, though. Boarded, shined floors. Circular tables that were crafted with white wood panels and had a smooth, polished end. Orange plastic chairs had plush cushions in various colors on them. At the windows, which extended to the floor, long tables were attached. There was a sofa near the right wall, underneath some admittedly ugly and dull-looking paintings. Curiously, she saw a few newspapers and some spoons and sachets of sugar in glasses. Greenery covered the spaces in between. The smell of cedar hit her nose. A little warm, a little too dark, but it seemed strangely normal.

A few doors lay near the back end. Four of them: two wide doors, identical, one on either side. One was narrow and lay behind a counter and had markings she couldn't quite make out. Farther back from the counter, deep in the shadows, were a set of two large, steel doors.

The counter was long and wooden. She noted the barrenness of it, the emptiness of the vast cabinet beside it. It seemed like one impervious wall.

There was a loud crash from behind the counter. A guy swore.

"A monster?" she whispered.

Out past the counter darted a small figure. Lucy gave a strangled cry—and then realized it was a cat.

Black, with strange white markings along its body, face, and tail, and big green eyes. It was incredibly fast. In moments, it was at her scuffed, broken shoes, sniffing at her heel.

Trying to quell her beating heart, Lucy beamed. Finally, something relatively normal here!

"*Don't move!*" yelled a guy. Lucy shrieked and nearly jumped out of her skin. The cat didn't seem to mind and just kept sniffing her.

Out from the back of the counter, another figure burst onto the floor. This time, though, it was a person. A young man with pitch-black hair, tired-looking eyes, a leather jacket, and a knife.

"What the heck?" Lucy nearly reeled back, but she didn't want to scare the cat. "Oh my god, don't stab me!" This place was going to kill her! Her voice echoed strangely with her panic, but she didn't move. *Strange. Even when I'm fearing for my life, I'm too busy trying to placate an animal.*

The young man with blue eyes and tanned skin shot her a peevish look, but he stopped. "Stab you? What the hell are you talking about? I'm trying to get rid of that thing so it doesn't kill you!"

"What?"

He advanced. "Just stay still. It's getting used to your scent. Don't touch it. I'll throw myself at it and hopefully this'll go through—"

"No! Don't kill a cat!"

His ice-blue eyes narrowed. "You don't know what that thing's capable of."

Okay, he was crazy. Time to get the cat and walk out of here. Smiling, Lucy crouched down in front of it. "Hey, little guy," she crooned. "Want a scratch? What's your name?" Gently, she petted it behind its left ear.

The cat looked up at her. Stared into her soul. Really stared into her soul, actually, she thought, really uncomfortably. Like it could see everything she'd ever done. And it was judgmental about it.

Then it raised its black-and-white-striated tail, maneuvered out of her pat expertly, and trotted off towards the back of the counter.

"Huh. It likes you," the guy said, watching it leave, entirely still holding the steak knife.

"Will you put that down? It was probably glad to see someone who wasn't going to butcher it." She got to her feet and regarded him as problematically as she dared.

He shrugged and tucked the knife away. Into his pocket, but it was something...she guessed. "Heh. Guess you might be able to survive this thing."

"Er, thanks."

"I'm John—"

A toilet flushed from somewhere out the back, and a girl strode into the darkened room. Lucy's heart fluttered in elation—she looked normal in comparison to the tired-eyed guy right next to her. Pink hair, brown skin, big, brown, doe-like eyes. She wore the same uniform as the one Lucy had been given. She analyzed the café as if she, too, were new to this.

"Nope. I'm still not dead and I'm still here. Bummer," she said with conviction.

"Yeah. Sorry," John said, shrugging and turning away from Lucy. "There's no escape here until morning now. It wouldn't unlock on time. The ca—"

"Doesn't matter now, does it?" the girl said, sighing.

Lucy didn't know which unnerved her more: The girl's words, the guy's words, or the fact that she wasn't running out the door. Clearing her throat, Lucy waved at the girl. "Uh, hi. I'm new here. Lucy. What's going on and who are you?"

"Tamara," the girl said dully. "...What job did he give you, anyway?"

"I'm the new barista."

Both the girl and the guy looked at each other. Lucy detected a hint of despair between them.

"How long have you two been working...um, here?"

"We've been here for five full days," Tamara said, rolling her eyes and sitting down at the nearest table. "This is our sixth. Woke up on a Wednesday, and it's almost been a week." Beside her, John looked dejectedly at the floor, as though he were considering ripping apart the boards with his bare hands.

"...Why does that sound like a warning?"

The two of them shared a look. Then Tamara promptly shrugged her shoulders, rested her cheek on her folded arms, and went to sleep.

Which left Lucy with the guy who'd pulled a weapon. Not all that comforting, she thought.

"Sorry about her," John said, as though he was the totally normal one. "She's always been like this ever since we woke up."

"Yeah, um...Well, put it this way, I'm not worried about her, exactly."

"What'd you say your name was? Lucy? Man, I haven't heard a normal name in a while."

"Which was five days ago..." Lucy wet her lips. "...Are you from *my world*?" She tried to tiptoe around *Earth*. Didn't want to freak them out too much.

"Yeah. I was travelling around Australia before I carked it. Was an engineering student before. And then I woke up in the interior." John's lips thinned to almost a line of thread. "And I've had to deal with this place ever since." He shook himself and adjusted his leather jacket—his trousers were dark and ripped, and his shirt was their uniform with the golden eye. "Tamara's from Spain, by the way. Ask her about it when she's awake next time."

"Oh." Right. Totally normal. "Um, so is there any chance we can find a way ou—"

Before she could finish her question, the door swung open, letting in a flash of light. Emil strode in, scowling.

As the boards were washed in bright sunlight, John slowly took out his knife.

"No!" Lucy cried. "You are not going after our boss with that!" In a smaller voice, she added quietly, "Until I understand what is going on!"

Apparently, this displeased the weapon-holder greatly. His eyes slid to her. "Don't you know what that guy i—?"

Something with intense velocity zoomed through the air and hit him on the temple. John crashed to the ground, groaning, the knife clattering to the floor. A coffee cup rolled away from him.

Did he just...?

"I brought snacks," Emil announced. The red jacket slung over his shoulder shone deep scarlet. Dumped a woven tray on a nearby table. "Eat, I guess." He clapped his hands, and the lights flicked on. There was a chandelier, Lucy noted. Surprising, and not allaying in the least.

The crackers were salted. There was dried cheese. Some plain biscuits. Really, Lucy wasn't that hungry.

By the time Lucy had nibbled at a few items, John had sat up, glaring—but not holding—daggers at Emil. Somewhere above them, a bell chimed out.

"Alright, that's eight o'clock," Emil said. "Pleasantries are over. We have work to do. Unfortunately, you two"—Even though he was wearing sunglasses, Lucy could tell he was looking between John and Tamara—"are still here, which means we need to open on time."

Tamara was sleeping, so what she would have said if she were awake remained a mystery. John looked like he was judging the distance between himself and Emil.

"And you aren't going to explain anything," Lucy said hollowly. "Are you?"

"Now that we've got a new barista, we're open for business," Emil said simply, as though that answered everything.

His reception: dull. John nodded shortly. Tamara slept. Lucy was just annoyed that everyone seemed to be skirting her questions.

"I'll leave this to you, Barista Girl," Emil said, handing the young woman a cream-colored apron. A red, embroidered eye on the left met her. "You told me you had experience in your previous establishment, so I'm leaving it up to you to work your magic and make drinks." He pointed to the counter and a rather clean-looking machine. "Changing rooms are to the side, not out back." Peeking out from the right wall was the small door. Lucy could now see it was decorated with the image of a human, a wheelchair, and a cat.

Not knowing what else to do, Lucy nodded.

"John! You're on bodyguard duty." Lucy's brows snapped together as John just shrugged agreement. "Tamara, you're a waitress. Keep doing what you're doing."

Tamara snored in response.

This place is a circus. How do we even make any money?

"This'll be our first day of business since *the incident* four days ago," Emil said.

Lucy was about to ask what *incident* that was, but by John's sour face, she decided it was probably better not to ask right now.

"Since we made some profit five days ago, the pop-up store isn't a complete bust just yet," Emil said. "However! We still need to make money today to keep it running. Lucy, it's all on you. Everything you need to know about the menu is overhead." He pointed to a giant chalkboard full of what looked to be squiggles. "You know what you're doing. You've got all the ingredients you need out back."

"You are an awful boss," Lucy muttered.

The man didn't listen to her. Instead, he turned to the door and drew a cigarette. "It's morning. You've got until sundown to make me some money. If this café goes bust...the three of you will regret it."

An ominous-sounding sentence. It was completely offset by him adjusting his jacket and announcing, "I'll be out for the day."

"You're just leaving us?" Lucy asked, mind still whirling. "After announcing that?"

Emil didn't answer. He was already out the door.

ESPRESSO MACHINE

After Emil left the building, his absence extended five minutes, ten. Lucy stood there in her new uniform and realized he was entirely serious and wasn't coming back.

His leave was expected, apparently. Nobody was making a move to exit the place, despite all the commotion beforehand. However...

"We've got two options," John said. "Now that you're here, you can help me by sharpening these pins." He'd taken off the buttons of his leather jacket. They were now incredibly pointy and incredibly unnecessary. "Or you can get acquainted with this map we drew up."

He jerked his head to the scrap of paper they'd apparently kept taped to the underside of the table Tamara still slept at. The paper was half-sodden with thick, dark marker lines. The pink-haired girl hadn't roused.

"I'll think about it," Lucy mumbled. She pretended to be preoccupied.

As she looked around the room, fumbling with the cuff of her shirt, she anxiously thought of her mother. She'd be worried sick about her, being dead and all. Lucy never would've thought that the afterlife would look so corporate.

Was it right to leave? Did they all have jobs in the afterlife? Emil had fed her...and revived her.

Seeing that Lucy wasn't going to help, John sighed and went back to sharpening the pins. Lucy spied the glass, double doors, and wondered what'd happen if she stepped outside.

"You're not taking this seriously, are you?"

Lucy glanced back at that. "What do you mean?"

"I don't know how to tell you this, but there's a spirit that's managing us this week. It's determined to stop us from making a profit. We're going to get killed if we're not careful."

Blinking, the young woman asked, "Are you serious?"

"Would I be carrying a weapon if I wasn't? Tonight's going to be difficult." He considered her. "Are you able to fight? Any experience in karate? Judo? Boxing?"

"I don't really think I can throw a punch." The words came out hollow.

"But you've got a survival instinct, I think." John smiled. Clearly, he meant it as a compliment. "You're tall. The cat didn't hurt you, either."

Now that she looked at him, there was distinctive bruising all along his face, his neck...

"...I can't fight," Lucy said quietly.

"No judgment, just, you know, seeing what we're working with. Oh, I know, you can use the broom." He nodded to the one that was kept spare by the counter.

"Okay, you've got to stop talking about ending things' lives." Lucy threw up her hands. "I can't take the thought of that right now! ...Why don't you just walk out the door?"

"What do you mean?"

"You're speaking like you're trapped."

"We are trapped."

Lucy looked to the door with absolutely nothing barring their way. "Emil's gone. This place is empty. We can go outside, right?"

She didn't believe in monsters, and she hadn't seen a sign of them anywhere. She half-suspected that John was...addled by his time here.

Without another word, she strode towards the door and the sunlight and the city outside.

"Hey—Barista Girl!"

Footsteps pounded as he followed after her.

She flung open the door and felt warmth along her face, heard the din of cars honking, and smelled the scent of petrol. Everything was normal, sunlit.

Nothing's keeping us here. She blinked at the fact. She thought of going back for them and telling them that, but she quelled it quickly. Something must have convinced them that they couldn't do this.

John was beside her, now, watching her. Almost willing her back inside, but intuition took over, and she inched closer to the edge of the awning.

Before her sneaker could clear the threshold between the awning's shadow and the normal sidewalk, John's hand was instantly on her shoulder.

"We can't leave past here," he said. His voice was clipped.

Something *was* wrong.

It was still a brilliant day, pure blue, sky-high buildings. People laughed, and Lucy could hear vehicles in the distance. But she didn't try to fight him off. The hairs on the nape of her neck were prickling.

Carefully, she looked around. Over her shoulder, back at the café. And she saw it on the pale brick wall.

A door on the exterior was open, right next to the normal door. This one was yawning wide and dark. A doll's hands were at the front, and something black began to ooze from the threshold.

Okay, clearly *that* wasn't there when she'd arrived with Emil.

Slowly, she stepped back, towards John. The entrance switched closed.

Silence.

"That thing was there?"

"The spirit said this: So long as we leave through the front door, that will follow us."

"So we're trapped here," she murmured.

"We found out the hard way," John said. He didn't offer anything more.

"How are you planning to get out of here?" Lucy made herself ask it.

"Our first idea was to draw up a map and escape. With a barista here, we don't have much time..." He trailed off, and Lucy tried to catch his eye, but he kept it trained on the door. "...There's another way. Let's see if you can make a coffee."

His face had darkened considerably.

Wait. Why does he look like that's the most disconcerting thing here?

*

Next to the espresso machine, with its back to the empty food cabinet, was a long, shining fridge. The pantry under the counter was bare, and Lucy found that all the ingredients she needed were chilled instead.

Syrups, powders and cocoa beans, and milk, all cold to the touch. An intense, overpowering, sugary scent of fake strawberries. Chocolate, esoteric, that wouldn't be out of place in an artisan's shop. The coffee beans, although chilled, seemed to be exactly the same as they were on Earth.

Okay. She could work with these. She had an idea of how to blend the flavors together, at least.

Which didn't take her mind off the fact that she was livid.

14

What was Emil thinking? He didn't tell me anything about that! ...Why a café, anyway? Surely no one's here because they want to be.

How have those two managed it?

She busied herself with trying to find her way around the counter.

The espresso machine was identical to the ones on Earth. Clean metal—a relief, and it looked like it'd been wiped down very recently, with an empty drip tray to boot. Maybe Emil took better care of this place than she thought he would have, monsters and all. Tentatively, she poured out some refrigerated beans and put them through the grinder. The machine hummed to life, and soon heat-infused espresso dripped through the portafilter.

"It works well enough," she said, more to herself than anything.

John watched her, elbows on the counter, silent. He was still wearing the leather jacket.

Figuring that she'd pry some information out of him, she began to speak over the whining. "I couldn't help but notice that Emil said you were the bodyguard."

"Yeah. I have to protect the furniture."

"You mean..."

"Tables, chairs, the lot of it. Stupid rule, but...that's what Emil's employing me for."

"So we actually get paid." Nod. "Even though there's a spirit that wants to kill us."

"Spirit manager," John corrected her.

The overhanging chandelier swung slightly. Lucy shrank from it, but as always, the café was empty with soft instrumentals played quietly through overhead speakers. As though no soul was around save for them. If the manager was here, they made no effort to make their presence known.

"Our checks are due tomorrow. What that means we can *buy*, I'm not exactly sure. But Emil will pay us. It's a thing."

Considering what was here, that was a surprise. So it was legitimately a job?

Lucy thought of the money at the end and cracked open a carton of milk. It was branded with telltale white and brown stripes. The liquid had a faint, almost almond scent to it.

She started to grind the beans.

"Emil. He's not crazy, right?" Her eyes flicked to John. "Like, this is actually a café where customers step inside. And it has...spirits and monsters. Which are real."

"Yeah, customers go in here all the time." A casual statement. "Emil's known around town, but it's not exactly for reasons you'd want to be known. Not that that makes any difference."

"The signs outside...And the newspaper..." It was next to her. She'd tried to figure out what it was saying, but even the pictures of buildings seemed to blend in together, indiscernible.

"It's a legit script. Tamara's working on deciphering it when she's not...out. Emil writes it on the boards outside, so we're guessing it's not total nonsense."

The wand whined.

I so want to get out of here.

"How have you and Tamara survived...?"

Her question was drowned out by the machine. Soon, the milk was silky, exactly how it'd look like back on Earth. She saw it was ready, and quickly she poured the steamed milk into the espresso.

She'd made a cappuccino. Born of practice, easy. The familiar fragrance wafted over them, and for a moment, the both of them were silent. Lucy remembered home...

"Just like back on Earth," John marveled, taking a closer look at the coffee. "Yeah, it feels weird seeing something that belongs back home here."

Lucy was about to ask again how they'd survived, but the boy looked like he was about to pass out on the counter. His lids were heavy. She decided she'd let him catch his breath. He looked like he'd been through hell.

Wait, is this Hell?

An overhead, brass bell tinkled. Alarmed, Lucy looked up. John blinked blearily. Must've been in a daydream.

Surprise hit her when she saw that an actual customer was walking into the café.

A portly man walked cautiously inside. He was dressed in office attire, with a thick blazer and slacks. His watery eyes flitted from the bland paintings inside to the counter, and he cleared his throat.

John muttered something.

"What's that?" Lucy whispered.

"Lucy—"

"Are you open again?"

Suddenly elated, sensing a small modicum of normalcy, Lucy perked up. "Um, hi! Yes, we're open." She didn't know anything about what was on the board, of course, but she decided she'd hope that he'd just order a normal coffee. Did they do those here? Or she'd just have to improvise, which *had* gotten her kicked out of university, but she liked to think that those were minor details. "What'll you have?"

The man paused as he looked up at the board. "Hm. What's on offer?"

"Well, I can make most coffees. So whatever you want. Take your time." *It's not like there's anyone else here to hold up in line.*

"That's the wrong thing to say," John hissed quickly.

"What do you mean?" Lucy whispered back.

"He'll dither."

Rude.

Thankfully, the man wasn't put off. He looked up at the board, tapping his chin thoughtfully.

They stood in silence as upbeat music played.

It *was* taking kind of long.

With every second that passed, John became more agitated. "Don't you see what's happening?"

"Why don't you just tell me what's happening instead of muttering about it?" Lucy hissed back.

"That man won't be able to make up his mind in time."

"In time for what?"

"You'll see."

ORDER

You may be confused as to why, with every passing second that the man delayed his order, John grew more irate. Lucy certainly was, eyeing the young man and noting with escalating worry that he looked like he was about to explode. Unfortunately, his incensed nature meant that he wasn't going to be able to tell her what was happening until it was too late.

To save a lot of time and a lot of guesswork, here is some information: The spirit that ran the café this week especially hated people who couldn't make up their mind when ordering a simple drink. In its evil mind, surely someone would have an idea of what to order *before* making their way into the shop. What if it were packed? They would hold up the line. It was inconsiderate, rude, selfish, and they'd rather be better off dead, were its feelings.

And they did die. Horribly.

None of this was relayed to Lucy, who looked awkwardly between John and the customer.

"What's in the caramel latte?" the man asked, gazing at the chalkboard of indecipherable words, tapping his round chin thoughtfully.

"Why don't you read the board?" John asked.

"Just checking." His eyes trailed along the flowing, swirled lines. Deliberated a little.

"Pick a drink! Any drink!" John said loudly.

Lucy squeaked, and he ignored her and added, "You should've thought about this before you walked in here!"

Thankfully, the customer seemed rather unperturbed. As though this kind of service was normal.

"Chill out," Lucy said to him under her breath, forcing a little smile. "Heaps of people do this, you know. We're going to lose a customer."

"He's dead anyway. He's going to get eaten."

He didn't go into detail.

The young woman blinked.

John swung to the man and yelled, *"Hurry!"*

In no hurry to make an order at all, the customer started to reread the lines he'd been focusing on. John looked like he was about to vault over the counter and drag him out.

Finally, the man opened his mouth to order, and Lucy's hand travelled to the cups to finally get going with work. "Okay, I'll have a–"

Before the man could finish his sentence, the sharp bang of a weighted door made Lucy jump. There was an awfully loud bark, somewhere between screaming and a guttural cry.

John swore and scrabbled across the counter, but something shot past him in the blink of an eye. Lucy saw a blur of pink, ragged skin and a figure as tall as her kneecaps. Powerful hind legs were covered in gray fur. It was the size of a medium dog, but it moved lithely, more akin to a lizard. That was all she managed to be cognizant of.

One moment, one glimpse. And then it reached the man.

John swung his hand out to cover her eyes. He couldn't quite reach her in time, though. What she saw, in great detail, was—

Redacted!

All that was left of the man was a torso. The beast gulped his head down past its long snout in a rather disgusting manner and kept his headless body pressed beneath its haunches.

Lucy's nails dug into her chest. There was no room to cry out. All she could do was note the blood, the quiet, upbeat ambience, and the silence it occupied. Note the dead *customer*.

They're real, she thought dimly. Those doll hands, Emil's warnings, these elusive monsters, they were real and not some kind of joke that her boss had concocted to get them to work.

"And that man is *dead*!" boomed a voice from somewhere on the loudspeakers. The sound was a warbled mix of the baritone of a man and the softness of someone still in their youth.

"Is that the spirit?" Lucy hissed, looking around quickly, skin crawling at the tone. It was vicious, too. Like its tone was made of sharpened daggers.

John was not paying attention to her.

"Great, there's all this mess!" Considerably less furious than when the customer was dithering over his order, John was scowling, grabbing the broom he'd kept close, and he strode over to the monster as its long snout reached for a table, and it prepared to bite down on the splintery surface. It opened its maws—

He raised the wooden handle high above his head and smashed it down onto the monster's head. "Don't eat the furniture!"

It hissed gutturally and retracted, then got up on its hind legs.

They circled one another. Meanwhile, the speakers overhead crackled to life once more. "Morning, new barista! I'd say it's nice to meet you, but I'd be lying. Welcome to your first and last day working for Emil. Try and clean this up."

Between the voice, the fight, and the body, she whimpered and felt like she was spinning even though she was stock still. "What *is* this place?"

"Lucy, could you get the mop? It might take two of us."

"No! At least explain to me what that voice was!"

"I'm kind of busy!" *Emil, what did you drag me into?*

…Why hasn't it decided to kill us yet?

The monster snapped at John, and she shrieked. He managed to twist away from it—apparently, he'd had experience doing this—and it turned easily on its hind legs.

Its brown eyes flickered onto Lucy, and she froze.

The eyes left her as John neared it.

Out. I need to get OUT.

John yelled and swung the broom down.

In the ensuing fight, Lucy kept her eye on the brawl and inched towards the table, where pink, cotton-candy-haired Tamara still slept at the table soundly.

Lucy tried to wake her by prodding her shoulder. When that didn't work, she shook her gently awake.

"Hngh." Long lashes fluttered. "What's happening?"

"Tamara, John's fighting to the death," Lucy hissed.

"What's new?" The girl's dark eyes watched the current battle. It would be difficult to say that either was winning, as the monster certainly wasn't cornered and John certainly wasn't giving up.

"This is just your standard day here," Tamara said. She looked ready to settle back down to sleep, but Lucy caught her.

"Oh no you don't!" The girl with the beanie glared at Tamara. "We should be getting out of here!" *I was freaking putting my life on the line to at least try and help you!*

"There's no escape." She rolled her eyes and let the unsaid *duh* hang in the air between them.

"Okay, so what do we *do*?"

"Personally, I'm waiting to die."

"Lucy!" John yelled it, and when she turned, she found *him* cornered. "The mop! Otherwise, this thing's going to bite through a chair!"

"You want me to fight with that thing over some furniture?" She looked to Tamara. "Is he serious—?"

Tamara was asleep, blissfully not hearing whatever Lucy had to complain about.

"Lucy!" John called. "We need to get the mop, the other broom, and a pan! We can't have a body on the floor again."

She didn't know why she didn't bolt out that door. Some freaked-out part of her just knew that they all had to be together, even if that meant dying with them. Where that intuition came from, she didn't know.

Just that she was here now, with monsters and spirits that were somehow real.

"Hurry!" John called.

She had only them. And they, her. *So you can't just leave him there.* They were kind words, but already a despair had fallen around her, and it was more out of numb helplessness that she went to the cupboard and retrieved the cleaning supplies. Her fingers moved stiffly, so stiffly.

I know I said I'd be brave, but...

Her mind was dredging up misery. This place was nowhere she could live. In the afterlife? Seriously? Still, she moved.

"Thanks," John called with relief as she crossed the counter with the supplies in hand. He was still fending off the monster.

She stared at the pink, torn beast, which was preoccupied, and then looked down at the boarded floor. Her eyes tracked to the trail of blood.

These two had been here for five full days, and they had not escaped. Maybe John was crazy because of it. And maybe Tamara...

Focus on the job. She was near the body, now. She just had to clean this. And then...

No, autopilot didn't think further than what it needed to.

Where was home? Was it far away? Was it even on this plane of existence? She wanted to find it again.

Her broken sneakers hit the body on the ground in her daze, and she blinked absentmindedly.

The monster felt the movement. This time, it turned to her easily, its brown eyes glaring. Up close, she could see the power in its jaws, and it reminded her of an unrestrained, possibly rabid pit bull minus any soul whatsoever.

Even though it was menacing, it did look like it was deliberating. Which was a plus, Lucy thought, forcing that positivity, except that it was deliberating in the way a crocodile might weigh up the two possibilities of either jumping up to catch a heron or maybe strike out at a zebra for its lunch.

Still, that was good—

The air bent around her, as though it couldn't withstand dithering nor sentimentality. In the blink of an eye, a figure had appeared before her.

It was thin and vaguely human-shaped, gaunt and stretched high. Its pallid skin flickered in and out, and the walls and boarded floor near it seemed to flicker with it, too. Its eyes were hollow, scribbled circles. Its mouth, which was black and white, flickered up and down.

That's definitely not a costume.

And it was right in front of her face.

Lucy was about to pass out when it spoke to her. This time, it sounded less warbled. More crisp and clear, like a letter you really wouldn't want to open.

"So, you're the new barista. I'm your spirit manager."

"How—How are you real?" she asked it.

At the sound of her voice and the look on her face, it shrank back and bared black and white teeth. "Yuck. Sentimentality. Disgusting!" Abruptly, it turned to the dog. "Bite her!" it commanded.

"What?"

John now looked a lot more unsure of his ability to smack things, considering that this was seemingly incorporeal and the monster was seemingly now disinterested in killing him or eating the furniture. Still, he took a swing at their manager.

Didn't do much. The head phased right through it, and the monster slipped past him and neared Lucy.

"Crud." Lucy took a step back, and it advanced. A crack sounded in the air as it broke the dead man's femur. "I—I don't want to fight."

Lucy stepped back as it advanced, but the spirit laughed and moved to the center to watch and said, "Hurt her!"

Clearly, talking things through with either of them wasn't going to work. Her attention tore from the spirit to the monster, and she thought frantically of how she could get out of this peacefully.

Her life had never been in danger. Her arguments were petty and sheltered. She'd never had to fight. Even when a dog had bitten her once, so long ago, she'd managed to pry herself free, and in the end she'd never had to hurt it.

"I've never harmed an animal," she admitted to it.

The air around them buzzed.

All at once, seemingly spurred on by the command, the monster lunged out and snapped at her hand. She pulled back sharply; its teeth gripped her left, and she felt warm, sharp weight and nettled pain.

She forgot that she was holding the mop, in all honesty. It practically moved of its own accord—one sharp strike against its cheek.

The impact thrummed through her hands. The monster let go. She'd never hit any animal before. Nor a person. And now it was their job?

"I hate it here," she said, voice small and cracking.

The mop had speckles of blood. She dearly missed home. The air went still. The command had stopped and all that was left was the pain.

The monster gave a screech and a howl. Something flickered in her mind, something of a girl running on a racetrack, and emotions rolled over her about being free and winning, and it meant something she didn't want to face. And then it dulled, leaving only her and the monster.

A tear dripped down her cheek. She didn't really want to cry at the end of her life, or her second life, all things considered. She considered herself happy, even with all the crud she had to put up with.

She'd never felt so alone. And she really couldn't fight.

"I want to go home," she said to it. "Do you understand?"

"Uh, I wouldn't be trying to have a conversation with it," John said. He'd managed to creep up behind it. Lazily, its tail lashed out at his hand, and he yelled and dropped the broom.

The monster watched her, and seemingly her tears. There was no spark of life in those flat eyes, and its gaze resembled nothing of any animal on Earth she knew. Cold, like a lizard's, and then somewhere colder beyond that. She was half-prepared for it to strike her again.

Then it turned on its back legs and vaulted off back past the counter. The doors to the back banged shut behind it.

Silence.

"Well, that was incredibly disappointing," the spirit said from behind the counter. "It only drew a bit of blood." She got the impression that it was rolling its eyes. Then it disappeared, leaving behind speakers that were still playing a jaunty tune.

Beyond the glass, people watched them from a distance. Their commotion in the café had actually drawn attention. Amongst the stares, Lucy realized she was bleeding along the palm of her hand. The broken mop lay askew on the floorboards, and dully she picked it up.

When she looked up again, everyone was walking past, going about their lives, and no one even so much as stepped foot near the door or looked their way again.

Honestly, I don't blame them. Why the heck does Emil let those things stay here?

"What just happened?" John asked, bringing her back to the present.

Lucy turned to him. "You're asking *me* that?"

"It ran away from you. How hard did you hit it?" When Lucy shrugged helplessly, not knowing what to think, John canted his head. "...Well, whatever. They're stronger at night." His face darkened. "Which is the problem."

It didn't take much to sense where the conversation was going. Lucy went to the counter, wanting to avoid both of the people she was trapped with. *I don't want to die here.* "It's about that spirit, I'm guessing. Also, can we get something for my hand?" She'd only just come to terms with the fact that monsters were real...so why not rip the plaster off and accept that a spirit was real, too?

Dimly, she pulled off her beanie to soak up the blood, but John waved her hand away and walked over with a surprisingly clean bandage. She noted that there was only one small bit of carton of milk left. Today was going to suck. But she heard John out.

"The reason we're not getting any customers...or the customers get turned away..." John avoided looking at the body. "...is that that spirit's been in charge since Tamara and I started. It's trying to maim us by any means necessary, and it won't let people through the door."

Lucy had questions about that—but knew now wasn't the time.

"If we don't have a profit at closing time, all the monsters and spirits in the *back*"—He pointed to the heavy double doors—"will come out and eat us. That's the eventual fate of all the people who work at Emil's café. The profit that's been made runs out tonight."

CHERRY CUP

John carefully wound the last of the bandage around Lucy's hand. She felt the thick fabric and its tension against her palm and thought deeply as nine o'clock hit.

"I'm glad I'm not alone," she said. Found herself saying it before she had even really processed the emotion.

Really, she did mean it. No matter how John and Tamara were, if she were here alone, she'd likely go crazy.

"There's a way to get out of here, you know. At least, that's the assumption. It's just hard to get to. We've marked it on the map."

He handed the scrawled-on piece of paper to Lucy. With her uninjured hand, she traced her long fingers against the black markings.

The map was of the front of the café. The back doors, the weighted ones behind the counter, were scribbled out in a hasty x. There were the staircases on both sides that she hadn't gone up nor seen. One of them was crossed out, as were the toilets. *No exit.* The windows, one by one, had the same treatment, along with a floorboard (They'd really tried everything). One spot, though, was circled. It appeared to be a room near the left staircase.

"It's a window," John explained. He rummaged through the pockets of his leather jacket. For the pins?

Instead, he procured an old, rusted key that was half the size of his palm. An ornate bow, relatively simple wards. It smelled of old metal.

Lucy looked up from it to him. "How did you get this?" she asked.

"That's a secret. There's a window we saw when we went up one of the staircases. Thing is, the door to it is often shut. And it seems like the only time it's open and available is during the morning, just before work. The monsters and spirits don't like us going near that staircase, either. Pretty big hint as to where we can get out, right?"

The young woman's brows drew up in surprise. "But that thing—"

"The spirit said that we couldn't leave through *that* door. From what I can gather, if you encounter a spirit, they'll try and confuse you, but they set limitations on themselves, and they're generally truthful. In a spiteful way."

Another thought came to her. "Were you guys going to—?"

"Before you came along, yeah. We were going to leave. I was probably going to have to carry Tamara out of there. She wouldn't have seen the point in trying to get up the staircase, not when things go wrong. Like this morning. I'm sure...when Emil employed us...there was a loophole."

"But you were still going for it. Why'd you stop?"

"Having a barista here complicates things." He shrugged. "There was a problem with the door, anyway, and I didn't want to leave you behind. Tamara would have to be carried out. And with Emil being there..."

So their only literal window of escape was gone. John still hadn't given up hope. There had to be a reason he was showing Lucy the key. She swiveled around to gaze at the scene beyond the sunlit windows.

People walked along the pavement on the far side, away from the café. "How many people realistically come in here a day?"

"We haven't had a barista in a while. But the one five days ago managed to get a decent amount of people in, according to himself. I'd say...seventy?" His jaw tensed as Lucy looked to him. "We, uh, did have another barista."

"Are they dead?" She only just kept her voice from squeaking.

"He's not here anymore." John waved her away. His piercing on his brow glinted. "Details."

Rubbing at her eyes, Lucy stood. She didn't know what she was going to do—other than yell at people from the window and get people to try their coffee. This was going to be the last day of her life? She couldn't have yet another letdown on her final day a second time.

For a while, Lucy was quiet as she stood near the door. *A rock and a hard place,* she thought. The sun warmed against her cheek. It reminded her of the weather that'd been there the day she died, and no longer was that feeling comforting.

Alone here, with monsters...

With Mikah long gone.

And Bernie, her dog.

And her mum...

John toed a fallen chair and set it upright, a remnant from the monster attack. He glanced at Lucy, saw her looking down at the floorboards, and said, "I know it sucks. And that it's scary. But you can't just stay there."

Lucy was silent for a moment. His words centered her. She clasped her hands together. "John, can I ask you about the monsters here?"

"Sure."

"Do you know anything about them? Why they're here?"

"Huh? Well...They've always been around. That's what Emil says, anyway. Not that I'd trust him."

Dubious, dark, but ultimately vague.

So he doesn't know. Lucy thought about that, then nodded, keeping quiet, looking at the warm, sun-washed boards. She remembered the lizard-like monster and took in a steady breath and wondered why she was the one out of the two of them who seemed to understand what they were.

"I've got some questions about this place," she said. "I need to know what's happening."

"Sure. Ask me anything." His reply was so normal.

Somewhat embarrassed by the tears she'd cried as he'd wound up her bite, she adjusted her beanie and set back her hair. "I will. And...please don't lie."

He blinked.

"What is this place?" she asked.

"The café's been here for ages. Emil owns it. No clue why we, of all people, have been dragged here to make a profit for him. Though I think he does employ humans for some messed up purpose." He sounded like he was testing her, but she didn't have the time to catch him on it.

"And the place outside?"

"No clue where it is. We might all be dead. All of us. That's my theory, anyway. Not everyone is aware of it. Like the customers." He looked up to the ceiling. "This might be punishment, Lucy."

"Punishment?"

"Yeah. For all the bad we've done."

Silence.

"Or maybe the afterlife is really screwed up. If this is even the afterlife at all."

"Have all the workers been dead people?"

"It's been too little time to tell. I'm assuming yes. You and the barista before you were both from Earth." At her look, he decided to tell her more. "On Wednesday, there was another barista employed with us. He got eaten four days ago." His face stilled, and he ran a pin between his fingers, clearly in unwanted memory.

She'd skirt that for now.

"We'll have to think of why we're all together," she said. "There must be something connecting us."

John nodded. Maybe he and Tamara had already guessed that. He saw her watching and half smiled. "Thinking that far ahead? I like your style." The unspoken addition: *We might not make it.*

"I wonder why it's a café, of all things."

"Does it mean anything to you?"

John's question took her by surprise. She opened her mouth to answer. All those emotions welled up on her tongue, and she didn't quite know how to say what she was going to say next, about making coffee for her mother and her course—

The bell tinkled.

Both turned around to look at a small figure, with a blonde ponytail, who had stepped inside and was now gazing at the still life paintings along the left wall by the couch.

Panic thrummed through Lucy, who glanced at the doors. *No way can I let those things eat this girl.*

No monster bolted out from behind the counter. It was just basic, bare music, and the three of them alone in the café.

John looked mildly annoyed at the interruption and completely out of his element. Lucy walked over and cleared her throat.

"Hi," she said, inching a bit closer to the potential customer.

The girl turned to her. "Hey. Are you still selling coffee? It looked like you were kinda busy." Her eyes tracked not-so-subtly to the remnants of Lucy's tears.

Lucy blinked. Her heart caught in her chest.

The girl standing there staring at her was shorter than her. Younger, fifteen. She had the exact same face as her best friend from high school.

But her friend—Anna—had died suddenly. And she was here, standing in front of her, arrested in time and fully *alive*. Lucy had grown, but the girl in front of her...

"Anna?" Lucy's lips barely moved as she said it.

The girl searched her face, and instead of the familiarity or that goofy grin, she frowned. "Uh, yeah?"

Exactly how she would've said it back then, scouse accent and all. "...Do you remember me?"

"Sorry, have we met? I don't remember you."

"I think we were friends, once. I'm all grown up now, but you..." When she saw the blank expression on the girl's face, she fell silent.

Realizing that this was all she was going to get—and that there were monsters here who would likely eat them if they stood around for too long—Lucy found her voice and said in a surprisingly even tone, "I'll get you a coffee. What would you like?"

If it was Anna, she'd say a cappuccino. They'd only had to stop at a fast food restaurant every Friday after school because Anna swore that they made the best ones. Lucy had always scrunched up her face wondered how her best friend could waste half of her allowance on a drink so nasty, of all things.

"A cappuccino," the girl said, looking at her like she'd grown two heads.

"I'll get that ready for you now." Lucy cleared the lump in her throat. "I...must've been mistaken. Sorry. I'm not that weird, promise."

Quickly, she made for the counter. John watched her, his lips in a thin line.

There was nothing to say to the girl who didn't remember her. They'd grown up together...yet she couldn't say anything to the girl. If Anna really did remember Lucy Vaudeville, Lucy certainly no longer looked like who she was in the past.

Lucy worked quickly. Her hands were deft. Anna walked up to her midway, and Lucy wondered if she was going to cancel her order, but the girl said, "Both of you look upset. It's kind of ruining the mood."

"This isn't exactly home." Lucy smiled it off. Cleansed her mind of all the wild questions she had, knowing that Anna wouldn't help her. When it came to give the girl her coffee, though, Lucy asked, "Why did you come in?"

"I really like the paintings."

Lucy paused, then nodded and handed her the coffee. When she'd been alive, Anna had wanted to be an artist. She was kinda bad at it...just like Lucy...but the dream was there. She'd loved kitsch ones. The plain realism framed on the walls wouldn't usually have inspired her.

Was the dream dead? Or did it not matter to her anymore? Did death change them?

Anna smiled and walked off with the coffee. Then she stopped and beelined back for the counter.

"Oops. You haven't charged me for it. A coffee's usually ten schmucks."

A blue, circular piece of paper lined with metal was pressed into Lucy's hand. She had no idea if it was the right change or not, but she smiled at Anna. Somehow, she stopped the smile from being watery.

"I hope you find your way home...but this place isn't so bad."

Lucy took the metal and paper. The girl walked away. Lucy saw her go for a second time, much happier...she just wished she wasn't so confused.

The door shut behind her.

The café returned to emptiness and music. Lucy left the counter and wiped at her eyes. Her tears wouldn't stop falling.

She was aware that John was looking at her. "Someone you knew?" A nod. "And she's supposed to be dead."

"Yes!"

"Sometimes they pop up."

He didn't explain further. Lucy couldn't make sense of it, and she knew that asking John about it wouldn't provide any clarity. Not knowing what to think, she sucked in a deep, tremoring breath and looked to the paintings that had drawn her old friend in.

They were kind of nice, she guessed, in an antiquated, classic way. Still, the style and the subject matter were mundane.

One of them caught her eye: a coffee cup decorated with red cherries. Like the one from her mother's house.

Quiet alarm made her step back, and it dawned on her what she was seeing.

Other paintings held her core memories in oil paint. Not all of them, but a lot. The gallery seemed to swim with them:

The view of the beach on a warm summer's day. A game of hide-and-seek when she was tiny. A small certificate of the barista course, tucked away in her old backpack. Among them, other paintings that weren't hers. She saw a boy with blue eyes and a girl who could only be Tamara. She stared at them, couldn't know what they meant. Why were these lining the café's walls?

"John," she whispered, "what is this place?"

The young man's silence was the only answer there.

INTERLUDE

The fragrant scent of coffee filled the kitchen, and Lucy twitched her nose as she poured steamed milk into a cappuccino cup dotted with cherries.

Even after all this time, she still had to adjust to the smell. She'd never been a big fan of espresso. Took after her dad in that way. To think that she was the one now making coffee in this household...

Warm light filtered through the French doors, light sweeping along the thrifted, patterned carpet. Her mother was curled up on the couch, filling in a crossword. Bernie, their white terrier, lay basking on the front porch. The lounge TV filled the room with chatter from a weather presenter—her mother insisted on switching it on every single day and never paying attention to any of it.

Picking up the cappuccino, Lucy carefully carried the drink over to her mother. Sat down on the opposite couch, the coffee table between them.

Her mother looked at the drink appraisingly. "How you make all these excellent coffees is beyond me, considering you don't even like them." Under her lashes, she regarded Lucy. "Unless your tastes have changed?"

Cappuccinos weren't her best work. It helped that her mother loved them. Lattes were her specialty.

Mainly because someone special had taught her how to make them first. Someone dreamy, with a handsome smile and eyes that made her mind go off track. Like right now. She shook herself a little and said, "Nope. Still can't stand the stuff."

"You have the palate of a five-year-old."

"Mum!"

"Oh, don't worry. You're *my* five-year-old. Always will be." Her mother reached over to pinch her cheek, and Lucy batted her away with the pillow. "Sappy enough for you?"

"Very."

"Now!" She rested the coffee cup down again. The cherry patterns flashed in the afternoon sun. "This job!"

Brief hesitation. Lucy dug her nails in.

"So...It's a dog walking gig—"

Her mother coughed. "What?"

"Dog walking—"

Coughing again, her mother said, "You can't be serious, dear."

Lucy's lip twitched. "What'd you expect me to say, nursing?"

"You could do anything!" Flicking through the paper, her mother said, "There's an administration job up at the hospital. Now, if I could get my friends to give you—"

"It won't work," Lucy cut in. Thoughts raced through her mind.

She'd already been to university—and been kicked out. She didn't fit in there. Or anywhere else. Her mother's friends had given her temp work, and there'd be that odd feeling of knowing that she wouldn't fit in no matter what she did, that the very essence of how she carried herself wasn't what they'd been looking for.

Not feeling like battling uphill all for a few months' work again, Lucy added, "I mean, it's something, right?"

"Don't be so blasé about this!"

"I'm good with animals." Which was the truth. Animals did love her. She nodded to Bernie out on the porch and added, "I can take our pet for walks, give him a friend to go with, and I'll get *paid* for it."

"You could be a veterinarian!"

Still with sky-high hopes and the faith that Lucy could handle scalpels and forceps.

"I can't do that." At her mother's look, she added, "I'll find another job to go with it. I just think, it's something—"

"I want you to set your sights high, Lucy. I don't want you to just think that what you do is just 'good enough'." At Lucy's look, she held her gaze to the ceiling and went on. "You can talk to anyone! You've been given a gift. There's no point in wasting it."

I'm worried about you, her face said.

You don't have to be, Lucy thought back. Thought of Mikah, who she'd be walking dogs with. It was his idea to get his boss to hire her.

They could do this.

I'll get my own place. I'll find my own way. I will, Mum.

She couldn't tell her mother that when she looked so angry, of course.

On that day a month before her death, she didn't want to relay any of that in that moment. She'd keep it light. "I'll never get a clerical job, and you'll have to drag me into a desk job and nail my hands to a computer." At her mother's scowl, she added, "It's not for me. You know that, right?"

Her mother watched her, and her face closed over.

Silence passed between them.

In her memories, Lucy had looked down at the coffee table between them. She remembered that reflection. Remembered how she'd felt that day. Remembered her mother's fear. Remembered that crushing disappointment.

Remembered that she hadn't made a coffee for her the afternoon she died.

I'm really sorry, Mum. Now I'm just hoping you're okay. I hope you're not worrying...and that I can reach you, somehow, from wherever I am right now...

MILK

"Tamara!"

Lucy shook her.

The girl mumbled something and her long, dark lashes fluttered open. She found Lucy standing over her, intent, and frowned. "Why did you wake me up when it's not even time to die?"

"Tamara, there are dead people we know out here," Lucy said quickly. "We need to find out why we're here and how that's happened!"

The girl stared at her.

"If we pool our knowledge together, maybe we can figure out why we've been transported here—"

"I'm not doing that." Tamara's lashes fluttered. She went back to sleep instantaneously, glad that this conversation was over.

Lucy peeled back from the sleeping girl. "There's got to be some clue between the three of us, and we need to work together. How come she zonks out all the time?"

"Her way of coping," John said, shrugging. He was standing beside her. "She's kind of in a different situation than us."

Lucy opened her mouth to say what she needed to—and felt her breath hitch.

Really, I'm just putting off telling John about the milk. Getting some probably involves fighting a monster or something. Still, I don't want to die here today.

"So...we're out of milk. Anna—the girl I knew—she had the last coffee." Lucy watched John carefully and fell into dismay when he procured the steak knife that he'd apparently recollected.

"We're going to have to go out *back*," he said.

"Of course you'd say that," Lucy murmured. As John stalked towards the large, weighted doors, she asked, "What about Tamara?"

"She'll be fine there."

"...And the customers?" Lucy muttered, but she supposed that didn't matter right now. Not to John or Tamara, nor perhaps Emil and the other creatures that resided here. She thought of the dog monster, shook herself, and followed the young man in the leather jacket.

He pushed them open.

Beyond the weighted doors, a cold draft clawed around Lucy's pinched face. A frigid loneliness emanated from the walls, and as she trailed John and walked inside, she heard inhuman screeches. The corridor was winding with seemingly many paths, expanding far beyond what the gray lighting could afford to cast.

"I'm never going to forgive Emil," she said to herself.

John nodded shortly, apparently in agreement. "Good, because you might have to fight when we get out of here."

I'm not doing that, but okay. Her eyes flicked to the beginning of the hallway.

The cat from before, the black one with strange white markings, was sitting there right near the entrance, staring up at her with wide, bright green eyes.

"Okay, little guy," Lucy said, inching towards it, "I can't let you die here. Come on, let's go back out front."

She attempted to scoop it up, but it dodged her hands and walked farther into the hallway. Down, down, until it was no longer visible.

"Come back!" Lucy cried.

"Don't worry about it," John said. "That thing's survival is the least of our worries."

Lucy shot him a judgmental look. He walked on.

Following him, she looked around at the all-encompassing shadows. "Thanks for coming out here with me."

"It makes things easier if there are two of us here."

"This place is certainly...claustrophobic."

"Tell me about it. The fridge is third on the right," John said. "Oh, and I should probably tell you about the looking back thing."

"...The looking back thing?"

"You've got to keep your eyes trained forward. If you want to turn back around for any reason, you need to find something in your periphery, focus on it, and turn while keeping it in your vision. It helps centre you."

"Otherwise...?"

"You end up somewhere deeper in the hallways. Or a spirit—there are multiple—can steal you away. Since you're our barista, we can't have you ending up lost or kidnapped."

"...Have you been out here before?"

"Yeah." No other answer. Lucy got the hint.

They got to the third door on the right, and Lucy sidestepped an embarrassing amount of trash and blinked as she found what appeared to be a blue Appenzeller sitting before a wooden door. The dog was held fast by a chain fixed to the wall. A bronze plaque sat above it to the right.

"This..."

"I know, I know. It looks like a spray-painted Appenzeller. But look closer."

Lucy did exactly that—and recoiled. "It's got no eyes."

Where they were supposed to be was simply a mass of shockingly blue fur. Its chain was not metal, but seemingly made of skin.

As if sensing her judgment, the dog began to bristle. Barked so loudly that it gave even Lucy, who'd worked with animals, a fright, and their part of the hallway reverberated.

"This is the fridge's guardian," John told her. "Its other half is inside."

"I don't really want to know what that means."

Disregarding her protest, John began to inch closer to it. The dog-monster began to growl, and another disconcerting bark rumbled through the hallways. Howls rose from further within the hallways in response. It lashed out at John, tethered only by the piece of skin, and Lucy sucked in a breath.

One magically engraved word appeared on the plaque behind the monster:

HAND

"The payment today...is someone's hand," John said through stiff lips.

"A payment?" Lucy raised a brow. Apparently, from John's tone, it was unavoidable. "I mean, can't we always find some other way to get the milk?"

"This is the only place that has it." John began to sweat. "Someone's hand? One of us is going to have to part with it. It's the only way."

"Isn't that excessive?"

"This place is excessive, if you haven't noticed."

"Well, we can't pay that. I'd rather make all the drinks without milk than do that."

Lucy looked to the dog-monster. Felt the same thing she did when the other one was out the front. A memory pressed just beyond her temple, a light stinging on her skin. For a moment, she saw a small, darkened room with the curtains drawn. Saw a girl taking in a deep breath and checking her phone. A mixture of two emotions, hope and the fear of being seen, feathered through her and made her heart pump faster.

It dissipated, and she felt herself being pulled back here. As though a hand had shoved her out of her own mind.

She looked around the floor at the random rubbish strewn around them. Saw a scrap of mirror, a stone, a twig.

"Fine," John was saying, pulling her out of her feelings. "...I'll do it."

She whipped around. "What?"

He was walking straight for it! "I'll give it my hand. If it's for us to survive one day longer, I'll do it. I've got faith in you, Lucy."

"You actually don't have to do that," Lucy said hastily. *Oh my gosh, I do* not *want someone to lose a hand because of me.*

Dramatically, he looked halfway over his shoulder. "Don't try and save me, of all people," he said in a low voice.

That decision was so fast! Where is his deliberation?

"I'll just try something first before you do that." Lucy really didn't want a lost hand on her conscience. She grabbed the piece of mirror and walked over to the dog-monster. It snapped at her, and its bark thrummed through the ground and jolted her bones. But she laid the piece of glass down next to it. Caught its reflection.

"Play," she said softly.

In an instant, it was much happier. The lock on the door let loose and the plaque blanked out.

John stared at her, open-mouthed.

"Um, thank you, though," Lucy said, adjusting her beanie and feeling incredibly awkward. "For trying to sacrifice your hand. It's a good thing you didn't need to."

They watched the monster nose around the glass, toying with it as a puppy would a ball. She wasn't sure about how safe that was, but hey, she was enjoying herself.

"...How did you do that?" John asked.

"I...saw another way?" Half-lying was nearly impossible for her.

"It listened to you," he said, considering this. "That's not normal. Last time, the barista had to sacrifice his hat. It hated him, and he couldn't do anything like that."

Lucy frowned. "Why is one day a hat, the other a hand?"

"How did you know how to do that?"

The real reason? The...monster...had wanted to see her reflection again. Lucy couldn't put it into words, though, so she decided to spin a half-truth on the fly. "It wanted something. When you want something but can't have it, you take something else as payment. That's why it's unlocked now, I think. There were a few things strewn around here, so I thought maybe they were there for a reason."

"I can't believe you could understand how that thing *felt*."

The Appenzeller-monster barked. The ground rumbled.

"It's not something. I think it's some*one*." Lucy's words were quiet. John frowned at her, not understanding what she'd just said. In all honesty, he thought she was speaking poetically. She did seem soulful.

Lucy got up, aware of his eyes on her. She walked over to the door and awkwardly waited, unsure.

"Milk should be straight through," John said, nodding.

The interior of the fridge was a strange, pleasant kind of cool that Lucy found herself unused to. As though this part was free of the terrible unease of the rest of the hallways. She wouldn't quite call it *peace*, but it was something of a reprieve. It was mostly empty, save for wooden walls, an overturned trolley, and a huge, vertical glass fridge full of cartons.

"You know, I think you're special or something." John tailed her, hands in the pockets of his ripped jeans.

Despite all that had just happened, she suddenly found herself back in her previous life. Not like the others? On the fringes even here? "I'm just me," she said quietly. All in all, she'd rather not be special here. Who knew what that would imply?

"You're not...sent by Emil?"

The question landed on her, and she almost turned back to look at him, but he quickly said, "Remember to keep things in your periphery out *back* when you turn!"

Holding her gaze forward, choosing instead to focus on the glass fridge, she asked, "Why do you think I'd be sent here by him?"

Deep down, she was hoping that John would still accept her. She didn't want to lose yet another connection, even one borne in near-death. She could never keep them. What would it say about her if she couldn't keep them in the afterlife, of all places?

"If you say you're not, I'll believe you," John said quickly, choosing to end the conversation. "I just...had to ask. Like you did out front. Yeah?"

Lucy nodded.

They reached the fridge rather easily. Lucy pulled the trolley upright and opened the glass to get to the hundreds of cartons, all in telltale cream and tan.

When she finished, John showed her how to turn around quickly enough without being whisked away.

"It does help with someone else here," Lucy said, laughing.

John smiled, though his eyes grew distant. Their walk back to the fridge's door was quiet, the woman trailing the young man, until Lucy spoke as she eyed the empty, spacious walls.

"I think that the monsters here were..."

She saw that John's shoulders were bowed. He must have been half-asleep, yet still, somehow, he was walking.

"Never mind," she said, sighing. They were almost out the door now, and she was just passing by a switch. She didn't know much about economics here, nor about paying rent, but she assumed that the light would need to be turned off.

So she flicked the light off.

The room fell into darkness. Immediately, John seemed to wake up from his daydream and said in a harsh voice, "Did you just turn that off?"

"Uh, yeah?"

"Don't panic. Just keep your eyes forward."

John searched for her wrist. Lucy let him take it, perturbed.

"What's so bad about—?"

Giant yellow eyes opened on all the walls, glowing in the dark and flickering. They were human, irises and pupils and all, crowding even the door to the exit. They flickered and pulsated, their edges grainy. All the pupils were fixed on her.

The monster's other half, Lucy thought vaguely through her terror. They matched what it was afraid of in real life.

As she stared, they began to move along the walls and cluster near her. The trolley jolted as she breathed quickly and picked up the pace. Outside, the dog-monster had stopped barking.

"Just keep walking forward," John said.

Something tapped her on the shoulder. It felt like a *person*. Yet John was in front of her.

Forgetting the iron-clad rule of not looking back, Lucy turned. One brief moment of forgetfulness and panic.

And she was gone.

Lucy's wrist disappeared from John's grip. He fumbled for her and swore. Realized that the dog-monster had stopped barking for a reason and that *it* must have been nearby when they were getting the milk. Taking a deep breath, he turned back, too.

And in an instant, the room inside the fridge was empty. The eyes blinked around the darkness, confused, and the blue dog-monster outside wagged its tail, chewing on a treat that its favorite spirit had given it.

SPIKE

Lucy spent some time in unconsciousness. Then she awoke to find herself lying on her side in the darkened hallway, head heavy and hurting.

Everything seemed further away, now. Just thin gray light and many, many doors in a hallway that seemed to extend forever. No exit in sight. Her throat was dry, and it felt like she had been out for quite a while.

"Ugh," she muttered intelligibly.

Her hand went to her side, and she went to push herself up—

She touched something cold. Even though it was solid, its presence felt...thin. Like cold, flimsy metal.

Blinking in the dust and the rubbish and the dark, Lucy looked up.

Her thin, gray, human-shaped manager was crouched next to her. Lowlight made its flickering skin look like it was phasing in and out of existence. The thin, hollow scribbles of its eyes were fixed on her. When her gaze fixed on it fully, its mouth split wide into a grin.

The shift from looking at John to something non-human was *not* what she wanted to experience upon waking up.

Lucy screeched. The speed at which she managed to scramble upright—well, she was sure it had broken a record. Now she was sitting up and scuttling as far away from it as she could. Her back hit a wall. Vaguely, she recognized John lying a few steps away, sprawled out and unconscious. The being cackled, and Lucy really wished she hadn't heard it laugh.

"Wh-What are we doing here, and why are you with us?" Lucy asked.

"So, you're awake!" it said, ignoring her question. Its voice made her uncomfortably cold.

Somehow, she made her voice steady and quiet. "What do you want?"

The scribbles on its eyes seemed to crinkle while its mouth elongated. Was that its genuine smile? "You spent a lot of time out," it said mockingly. "It's almost eleven, in fact."

Alarm panged through her veins. This being clearly didn't care if she stayed longer. "Why did you get that monster to bite my hand?"

"I wanted to say hello to Emil's new barista," it said mockingly, ignoring her question. "Personally. And it seems that I caught you taking an extended break."

Lucy felt something give way under her left leg. She yelped, pulled it back, and spikes shot up from where she had lain only a few moments ago.

The monster laughed hideously. Lucy stayed open-mouthed, looking at extremely sharp spikes.

"That...would've killed me," she murmured. More to herself than to the other thing here.

"That was the point, idiot," the monster said brightly. "I see Emil is only employing the best and the brightest."

"Why?! Why would you do that?!" Realization was slowly dawning on her.

"That's how it works around here," it said in a casual tone. "We spirits cannot kill you—not outright until the end of the day when you haven't made a profit. The spikes would have merely maimed you. But we *can* do something like this." It nodded to the remnants of the trap. "Or oversee the café and make sure all the customers die."

Quickly, Lucy scrambled up and dove for John and shook him. "John, I need you to wake up right now!"

The young man's blue eyes opened and locked on the spirit. Was that another bruise? But he asked her, "Are you alright?"

"I'm fine." She didn't think he could do much about it anyway.

Lucy noted that the spirit was waiting patiently. Because they were wasting time? John had no cuts, which was good. Summoning her courage, she got to her feet again. "If it's nearly eleven...then we need to get going."

The spirit laughed as she looked around. "You don't even know what will happen, do you, human?"

A few feet away, she spied her trolley still full of milk. That'd been relocated just a bit behind their side of the hallway, too, which made her uneasy. "Why us?"

"Why not?" The spirit looked down at John. "He turned around as well, so I was able to steal both of you away."

"This is entirely unfair." She couldn't believe she was complaining to something that harbored her ill will.

"That's the point!" It laughed that fake, hideous laugh. Then it went silent.

Not knowing if what she was doing was smart or not, Lucy kept it in her field of vision but went for the cart. She went to pull the trolley out of its corner—and found that the wheels were now padlocked with steel.

Seriously?

The spirit got to its full height—nearly Emil's—and closed in on her, reminding her of a flickering wraith. She froze. When it got close to her, though, it merely waved a key in front of her face. "I've got the one for the lock," it said simply.

Lucy grabbed a milk carton. "I guess I'd just need one or two."

"Do you really think you can serve enough customers with one or two cartons? Surely you don't want to go out the back again. You'll have to face the monster inside the fridge again. And me. And next time, my traps won't miss."

John had crept up behind it. Went for his knife—and frowned as he came up empty.

"I confiscated it," the spirit said over its shoulder, bored. "But you can keep the pins. They're stupid enough that it suits you."

The young woman thinned her lips. "What do you want?"

"Do you want to see the previous barista?" it asked. "If you come along and see him, I'll give you the key to the trolley. Then you'll be free to go back out the front."

"Don't," John murmured. In the light, he'd paled.

It threw her a smug, ugly grin that split its face. Lucy stared back—then shrugged. "Where is he?" she asked, because in truth, she did want to know.

"A few doors down," the spirit said. It started ambling away, its gray, pallid skin shimmering like a ghost's, and Lucy bit her lip, left the cart, and followed it. She tried to appear careless. Deep down, her heart hammered in her chest.

Their footsteps mingled. They passed only a few other doors, some with a sheen of what could have been blood but might have been coffee. John said nothing beside her, his head bowed. A monster screeched from somewhere close by. Nothing appeared in the hallway.

"What is this thing?" Lucy whispered back to John.

"It's in charge of us for the week," John said. "Spirits are supposed to be worse than monsters. They can think, rather than act on instinct. That's all I really know about it, for all it talks about itself. Just our luck, it's apparently the most bloodthirsty spirit here. According to itself, of course."

"...I'm sorry, but I needed to see this."

"Can't fault you for wanting to see the barista. But just be prepared for what you see."

They passed by an open door with many glass cases. John walked right by it and apparently didn't see anything of note, but Lucy blinked.

The spirit threw open a narrow, inconspicuous door right next to the one with the glass cases.

"Wait." Lucy pointed to the cases in the room next to her and John. "What are those?"

John frowned. "It's just an empty room."

No, it definitely wasn't empty. She could see old equipment in there, most of what appeared to be junk, locked inside separate glass cases. There was an overturned cart there with a bite mark in it, almost obscured by a broken jukebox.

The spirit sighed. "All baristas see things that other workers can't. You're a bit like a spirit or a monster, only far less capable. That makes sense, doesn't it?"

Seeing that John was looking into the room in confusion, then to her, Lucy pressed her lips together. Neither of them could—or would—give her a straight answer!

The spirit waved her towards the door that it was interested in. Lucy stepped forward and looked inside. John stepped back, arms folded, as though he already knew what was there.

Vast darkness. The humming of a fan from above. Somewhere in the dim light, she saw...a cupboard. One big, long, vertical cupboard that extended higher than she could see. The latest ones at the bottom were yellow shoes, men's nines.

"Why are you showing me..."

"Those are his shoes!" The spirit smiled at her. Its grin was hideous. "It's all that's left of him, of them, after we killed and ate them!"

Silence.

"How is showing me their *shoes* going to do anything?" Lucy said. Her voice was level. Behind her back, her fist was clenched tight, and she was sure that if her fingernails had been any longer, she would be drawing blood.

The spirit, too, was not fooled. "You fear death," it said casually, "because you have felt it before. And it changed you, didn't it?" Lucy remembered the feeling of the ending of her previous life and flinched just a little. "It scares you more than anything! But what can you do? Look at how many shoes we have collected…Give it to Emil to leave all of them here wedged away in a tiny little cupboard room. They give a café all they've got, since their lives depend on it, and they're just left here as hideous plimsolls. I mean, that's the workforce, isn't it? Emil's no different than a normal boss, really."

It clearly loved the sound of its own voice.

"What's your point?" Lucy asked.

"My point…" It rounded on her. "…is that this is all you'll be. I've seen humans look me in the face and laugh. But they don't laugh when their profit is gone. It's a terrible café to run. And I want you out of my sight."

Lucy considered this.

Might as well try this.

"We don't want to be here any more than you want us to be here," she said. Unlike the monsters, she couldn't tell what emotions were coming from the spirit, or what the spirit was exactly. But she had to try. The pain in her bitten hand and John's presence centred her. "We all want out."

The scribbled eyes narrowed. "What are you trying to do?"

"If we make a profit today, we want to go," Lucy said. "All three of us. We don't want to go back to the café. As soon as we win, we'll quit. We'll only work one more day. Then you can be free of us."

The spirit stared at her.

"Are you trying to bargain with me?"

"…Yes."

It considered this.

Then it let out a hideous laugh that went on for ages and ages.

Disconcerted, Lucy looked to John. His eyes were glued to the spirit that was still laughing.

Eventually, it died down. The spirit cocked its wavering head at Lucy. "Nobody told you?" it asked mockingly.

"Tell me what?" Lucy asked.

John bowed his head.

"Emil employs all the lost little humans who died in their world and woke up here for fodder," the spirit sneered. "Every night, we would be able to get out if it weren't for the profit that keeps us in the shop. If that fails, the employees are the sacrifice that keeps us in this establishment. In exchange for your failed lives, the rest of the city can be free from us. There is no escape. Your purpose is to die here!"

Lucy's jaw nearly hit the floor. She nearly whipped around to look at John, then remembered the no-looking-back rule, and asked, "Did you know this?!"

"We found out on our first day. I thought you knew."

"Well, it was the bloody wrong time to find out!"

She heard the spirit snicker, and she carefully looked back. Faced the truth squarely.

"...You're trying to kill us this time by..."

"Telling you to give up." The spirit shrugged its thin, looming shoulder. "It'll save you a lot of heartache." Brightly, it added, "Oh, and it works, too. Telling humans to give up. Why would you keep going, knowing all this?"

Lucy looked to the shoes. They were neatly stacked, tidily put away. In this dingy, dark cupboard, with maybe-blood spatter, maybe-coffee stains.

"I have to go," she said thickly.

The spirit looked after her as she went. It knew, just a little, that it had won.

Which meant it was time to rub its victory in her face.

KEY

At the front of the café at half past eleven, things were now a little different.

Two customers stood near the counter. The one in front mulled over her order. They'd come in despite the altered ambience and the spirit standing right next to Lucy. Apparently, they didn't even register the spirit as anything but a worker here.

There was a very long wait for their order.

The woman at the front tilted her head, reading the board. "Can I ask what's in the strawberry—?"

The spirit waved its pointed hand. A trap promptly erupted from under both of them, and, well, the result wasn't pretty.

"Decide on what you want before you go up to order," it said, sniffing despite its lack of nostrils. "Your inconsideration is despicable."

Its trap had killed the customer behind the woman as well. The spikes retracted. As they did, they hit one of the tables, nearly knocked it over. John yelled, dropped cleaning supplies, and dived for it. Saved it from tipping just in time. "Watch where you put those things!"

He'd had a lot of work to do. Four people in total had made their way into the shop since the spirit picked up its shift out front in the café, and all had paid dearly for it. That meant cleaning the bodies and ensuring blood didn't get on the furniture.

Tamara sat there, awake and sweating, nervously eyeing the spirit. She muttered something about getting possessed.

Bored, the spirit sat on the counter as upbeat music played. "You three are draining this place of its energy. This floor has more charisma than the entire team."

Lucy couldn't contain herself any longer. "How are we supposed to make any money with you killing all our customers?" she burst out.

The spirit looked into the fridge, its mouth in a flat line. Was it grimacing? "I'm the one who should be complaining. I have to be stuck with you for another four and a half hours." It smirked as it looked back at the dead bodies in the reflection on the floor. "Still, at least *I* can make things interesting. Humans are no fun."

"This isn't fair," Lucy muttered.

The spirit considered this. Looked pensive. Then its expression lit up. "Oh, I know. You three can help me with target practice."

Where the chandelier had once been, a swinging axe now undulated. Pink eyes glared from behind the boarded walls. All the paintings had gone dark and murky. If it could interior decorate with just a thought, Lucy didn't want to see what it could conjure up with target practice.

Tamara turned a little green.

John cracked his knuckles. "It'd be my pleasure to gouge your eyes out." It didn't have eyes, but his sentiment was appreciated.

Lucy, however, sighed.

"Just leave us alone until our time is up," she said. "I don't know why you're out here."

Its scribbled eyes narrowed. "Because something's *up* about you."

Lucy frowned—and saw that John and Tamara were now paying attention.

"I've been murdering humans left, right, and center for a long time here," the spirit said. "There's something about you that really ticks me off, and I don't know why. So I intend to kill everyone who steps through this door to be rid of you."

Heart prickling, Lucy scowled.

The bell jingled. Someone stepped inside.

The spirit turned greedily. "Including this—" Its shoulders slackened. "Oh. Emil."

Lucy let out a breath that was full of conflict. Relief at the prospect of not having to witness more senseless violence. Disappointment that her new boss, of all people, wouldn't get an axe to the face.

"What's going on here?" Emil demanded.

The spirit gave the impression that it was rolling its eyes. "I just changed the atmosphere. All of these employees are so dreadfully boring!"

"I'm here, so you're relieved of your duties," Emil said. "And give me my keys back. Also, get off the counter."

"I like it out here," the spirit said, sniffing. Seriously, how was it doing that?

"You can manage them any way you like," Emil said. "However, I need some space to do my paperwork."

He was holding a newspaper.

That relief and disappointment Lucy felt quickly gave way to one emotion: anger. How dare he treat them like a commodity! He wasn't even concerned about the bodies that John was struggling to clean up.

The spirit muttered something about not giving the keys back and disappeared. Silence extended. John watched Emil under his lashes.

Lucy waited one moment. Two.

Emil glanced at Tamara, saw that she was trying to get back to sleep, and said, "This place is a mess. Also, ten schmucks? Seriously?"

"You *tricked us!*" Lucy exclaimed, storming past the counter and striding up to him. "You tricked *me!* You made me walk in here and employed me just so I'd die! How dare you! You trapped us all in here with a spirit of all things—"

"Language," Emil said.

"Oh, sorry, but I don't give a crud!" Tears pricked at the corners of her eyes. "My life was finally looking up when I suddenly died. I've only been here three hours and I'm already going loopy! Do you know that I feel sadness radiating from the counter? Sadness? Since when does a counter have an emotion? I'd rather be at peace than work here! Why did you do this to all of us?"

Emil was quiet.

"I've seen what happens to the baristas and the other workers, and I've seen why there are monsters here!" Lucy went on. "The spirit told us we were sacrifices for some bunk city that doesn't even make sense. I haven't even been here that long and I know way too much. The monsters are the people from this city who died in this café. *And* I get their memories in my head!"

John blanched and looked down at the mess he was currently cleaning up. He needn't worry, though. All their souls travelled out the back, reformed with the urge to act on an instinct based on what they were like in their previous lives, and they put on a nice new coat. It was an almost entirely clean process.

"No wonder there are so many of them," he muttered.

"And you employed me!" Lucy nearly punched Emil, who was still just standing there. "What were you thinking? Why do we have to *die* here?"

Emil's face was extremely straight. Not one word she'd said was reaching him—or at least it seemed that way. Maybe he was just ticked off.

"Stop assuming that I'm here to make you die," he told her.

"What?"

"You can still make a profit today. You know that, right?"

"Huh?"

"I've employed plenty of people before." Which, really, was full of implications that Lucy didn't really want to think about. "Many of them gave up. But a lot of them made it through their first day. I don't see why you can't be any different."

Lucy paused at this. Of all the things Emil could have said to her, she didn't really expect it to be encouragement.

"Those two are a different case, though," Emil said, pointing to Tamara and John. "They're definitely toast if you don't figure something out." The two slept and scowled respectively.

"How do you know I can make it? How do I do that? Someone needs to tell me what to do."

"How do I know you can make it...? Well, I don't know exactly what you're going to do." His voice amped up again. "My advice would be to W-O-R-K. Seriously, ten schmucks?"

Offended, Lucy scowled. "We can't leave, though!"

"Yes, you can... If you want to work and not LEAVE."

"Are you serious?! Why didn't you tell us that before you left!"

"I'm a manager, not a babysitter."

"Our spirit manager thing told us we couldn't! It's supposed to be truthful!"

"Yeah, you couldn't LEAVE if you wanted to just shirk your shift. But you can still do your job and exit. Neither I, nor it, have to tell you that. That's simple business rules."

"You're costing your business money by not telling us that!"

Emil pursed his lips. "Don't tell me how to run my café," he said amongst the dead bodies. "This establishment is doing fine." Conversation over.

Frustrated, Lucy turned from him, fuming. *This place is a dive, but whatever.* She dodged the swinging axe and went back to the counter to think about it—

And then turned back around. "Can I have the key to the coffee cart out *back*?" she asked carefully. He'd been thumbing through that cluttered key chain when she was about to enter the café and gain employment.

"I don't have that key anymore."

"...The spirit took it, didn't it."

Arguing with it was the last thing she wanted to do. Time was of the essence, though, so she cleared her throat, spun around to face the glaring, pink eyes between the boards in the wall, and knocked on the wood, figuring that would get its attention no matter where it was.

The pink eyes undulated and then squinted. Lucy sucked in a breath, and the spirit appeared before her, ticked off.

"What?" it demanded.

She drew in a deep breath. "Could I have the key to the coffee cart in that case?"

It glared at her with its hollows. Lucy got the feeling that Emil's presence was keeping it from trying to harm her...

Never mind. He was flicking through the newspaper, turning away from their conversation so that they didn't bother him.

"We need to use the cart if you're just going to maim all the people who walk in here," Lucy said. "And the way this place is set up now? No one's going to want to come here."

The spirit's face split into a sneer. "Fine. I *can* give you the key."

Lucy's heart soared.

"So long as you do something for me," the spirit said, and her own soaring one suddenly floated back down to the figurative ground, much more sober and aware. "You like taming the monsters here, don't you?"

"One of them bit me. I'd hardly call that enjoyable." Her head began to hurt.

"If you prove your mettle by going into the second door on the right, I'll give you the key."

"There's something that's going to kill me, isn't there?" she asked it.

It smiled at her.

Emil turned over the page of his newspaper.

Lucy had one thought running through her head:

I am so dead.

TRIAL

As Lucy opened the weighted double doors, an image flickered through her mind. By now, she was used to the sensation. It'd had the bad habit of popping up, and its invasive nature still wasn't welcome when she was trying to focus.

In her mind, an impossibly big, ape-like creature with what seemed to be razor blades as its shell hulked inside a vast room. It took up *all* of the massive space it was in. Its maw had jutted teeth. And it watched the entrance to the room intently, its mind on killing.

The vision disappeared. Lucy realized she was still standing there with her hand clasped around the handle of the double doors.

"You okay?" John was standing by her now, hand on her shoulder, looking concerned.

"She's fine," said the spirit. "Unless you want to tap out?"

"I'm fine," Lucy coughed. Threw John a smile and walked into the hallways.

Cool draft, gray light, winding doorways. She shivered in the cold and took a step forward as the spirit was bragging about something to John. She let the doors close and took in a deep breath. Then she saw movement.

The cat was now sitting at the entry point. Black fur, white markings, green eyes, staring at her.

In the short time she'd been here, it'd been like her little guardian animal to let her know everything was all right. She'd grown attached to it in the way that life-or-death situations tended to bring forth.

"Seriously, you've got to get out of here," she said. At its otherworldly stare, she added, "This might be the last time I see you. I don't know how to tell you this, but there's a huge monster residing in the second door, and it wants to fight me, and it's got opposable thumbs. And I don't want to fight it, and I'm all about peace, you know?"

The cat stared at her.

"So you've got to get out of here," she added.

She went to scoop it up, but—

It jumped out of her two-armed embrace, walked straight towards the second door, and squeezed inside the impossibly small gap under the door.

Covering her mouth to stifle her squeak of horror, Lucy stared at the door. No sound followed, but that animal had surely just *died*.

Her conscience was screwed.

Then the spirit threw open the weighted double doors, and Lucy gritted her teeth as it strode in and said, "Follow me, human!"

John barreled in. "I'm going with you."

Knowing there was nothing else she could do, Lucy followed. It seemed forever before they got to the door, even though it was right near them.

The second door was vast. From what she could gather, the interior beyond was vaster. A small engraved image lay on a golden plaque: an ape with razor blades jutting from its back. Broken skulls lined the spikes. Classy. Although, as she regarded the engraving, Lucy was far more concerned with the gap in the door and the cat that'd scarpered through it than the fact she'd have to fight this thing.

"You think you're so great with your abilities," the spirit said hatefully.

Lucy scowled. She didn't know if knowing the pasts of the monsters and seeing the coffee cart was good or bad, considering that they were the reason she was now about to go inside this room.

"So why don't we see how you tame this monster?" the spirit continued. "Pumpkin Soup is one of our oldest monsters—"

"Pumpkin Soup?"

The spirit wavered. "Yes. Pumpkin Soup."

Ah. So that was what John had meant when he was talking about *normal* names.

"And he's been stewing in hate since his inception," the spirit added, cutting her a withering, scribbled glare. "Anyone who walks into his lair is dead meat. He wants to kill thirty workers—oh, don't look at me like that, he kills them only once four o'clock hits. Follows the rules and everything—for training, and then he'll open his door and fight the other monsters. You'll be his twenty-fifth worker."

Obviously, they didn't want that to happen. She hadn't noticed it before, but a deadly aura emanated from behind the door. A pure killer instinct. Even John looked hesitant to go through. Obviously, she was the one who had asked to do this, so...she'd do it. Besides, that cat was really weighing on her mind.

She touched the handle and took in a deep breath.

The spirit laughed. "Oh, you really are brave."

Maybe this was about facing her fears. Maybe the afterlife was all about learning some kind of emotional lesson or some bunk. She searched her heart and found one emotion that could push her forward. *Mum, you'd want me to do this, wouldn't you? You'd want me to be brave, wouldn't you?*

Actually, not really. If Lucy's mother were here, she would have done anything but let her daughter go through that door and fight something seventy times larger than her. But that was beside the point.

Lucy sucked in a deep breath. Scrunched her eyes shut.

Pulled it open.

Felt the killing aura.

The spirit pushed her inside, and she fell forward before she was even ready. She let out a yell, and her eyes flew open as she frantically looked up and steadied herself, and it laughed.

Then she frowned.

There was no monster there.

Instead, a cat with white markings sat in the middle of a vast puddle of what was definitely blood, cleaning its hind leg.

Did that cat just...?

"*What?*" yelled the spirit, pushing Lucy aside. She yelled out, and John caught her before she could fall. "That's impossible!"

"It's dead," Lucy exclaimed.

"No ♦♒)(♦📫," the spirit snapped back. At its second word, the air seemed to warp, and a buzzing sound popped in her ears. Lucy was entirely unconcerned with this abnormality and regarded the cat in amazement.

"Dude, you are a total freak," she told it. "An amazing freak of nature."

The spirit aimlessly drifted towards the walls and stared at the blood. Its face could only be described as ashen. Then it glared down at the cat, which by now was licking its paws and maybe settling down to have a nap. "Affogato, what the ✗♦♍&⌐📫? Do you know what you've done?"

It nearly choked on its non-existent vocal tract as the cat walked over and rubbed its face against its spindly left leg.

Disgusted and mortified—and embarrassed, because accidentally not maiming your opponents does tend to upset one's afternoon plans—the spirit stared uncomfortably down at it. "You...actually care for this human. Yet you're a cat."

Lucy was just staring there. Peacefully. The spirit sensed this, and, enraged, it turned to her. "You!" It yelled, pointing. "You cheated!"

"Cheated?" she cried.

"You got Affogato to fight your battles for you!"

"No I didn't!"

"Something else!" it cried quickly. "You must do something else!" It struggled to think of anything that wouldn't involve someone being maimed nearly to death, but eventually it settled on, "You must make a coffee and prove to me that you're a good barista. And if you fail, I will be holding my target practice on time at four o'clock."

Lucy's face pinched, and it smiled smugly to itself. With Emil's employees' track record, it doubted she'd be able to sit anywhere above terrible.

*

All eyes were on her in the front of the café. Tamara was awake again, nervously fidgeting with her hair clips. Emil watched from over his newspaper. John folded his arms near the counter. The spirit was close, very close, scowling. The axe above them swung very, very fast.

No pressure.

"By the way," the spirit added. "That coffee cart is more trouble than it's worth. Trust me, you don't want it."

Wordlessly, she started on her coffee. She hadn't actually made many of them during her time here, all things considered. Her fear now was that she'd drop the cup, or she'd be distracted by the eyes, the situation, or the spirit practically fake-breathing down her neck.

Yet she forgot everything bad. In that moment, she remembered why she'd even wanted to become a barista. The reasons were all so mundane but so important. To impress the guy she liked. To make a coffee for her mother. Because it reminded her of sitting out on the porch with her dog on rainy days.

Because it felt like home.

Almost in an instant, it was over. Time had gone so smoothly and quickly, and she poured the last of the milk into the cup.

She'd made a latte. Her best drink, exactly the way her crush had taught her to make it, the way she'd always made it.

All was silent. Tamara and John held their breath in tension. Emil watched the cup, expressionless.

The spirit...

56

The spirit's scribbled eyes looked two times bigger as it stared at the latte.

Then it vanished. Two keys lay on the counter: The first, rose-gold and heavy-looking. The second was small and blue and sparkly.

"Huh. It didn't even try it."

A slew of emotions rolled around in Lucy's stomach. She'd done it. She'd made a good coffee—that was their condition, right? So that meant she was capable of this, even by monsterland standards. She'd won!

She also knew that time was of the essence. So she grabbed the two keys, pocketed them, and went to retrieve the cart.

COFFEE CART

It was now twelve o'clock.

Lucy wheeled the bitten coffee cart to the front of the café. In the end, it'd only required the heavy, rose-gold key to unlock its gigantic case. She'd tried a few more glass boxes with the tiny, sparkly key, but nothing in the room seemed to fit it, and there were so many it'd probably take her the better part of the afternoon to test them all. Maybe the spirit had left it to mess with her. That seemed to be its modus operandi.

In any case, the blue, sparkling key now rested in the pocket of her trousers.

John messed around with the generator, then kicked it. Lucy wasn't sure how wise that was, but he was the engineer, not her, so she'd trust him. Effective, too, because after that, the coffee cart hummed to life. She whooped with excitement when she saw the surprisingly spacious fridge in the lower corner flick on—and got the distinct impression of wanting to shut herself away from the world, which quickly passed. This ugly, bright yellow, beaten-up cart with chew marks and a piece of wood hastily taped to the overhanging front was already growing on her.

John killed the generator, and upbeat music replaced its hum. "We got lucky," he admitted. "The generator's main wire won't budge no matter how much I try to get behind it. It's hooked in tight. Good thing that everything's running now, though, right?"

Tamara, surprisingly, stood beside them. It was strange *not* seeing her asleep. Her doe-like eyes flitted around the room, but she kept near Lucy as the latter grabbed coffee cups and milk.

"You've got to listen to me, because I've figured out how all the money works here." Tamara leafed through a thin notebook she'd kept and began writing on the pages. "I don't have much time."

That attitude mirrored exactly what Lucy thought. Even with this stroke of luck, it still looked bleak. Lucy didn't know how they were going to pull through, but she had to say something, anything, if only to allay herself.

"We'll get through this," she said, determined. "We only have to get through today, and then we'll find a way out." John had that key of his own.

The pink-haired girl blinked. "Oh. Yeah, no, I wasn't talking about death or anything." Looking away, she added in a mutter, "That's probably going to happen no matter what."

Before Lucy could say anything, Tamara spoke again.

"No, what I'm talking about is something...different." The girl suddenly sounded a lot younger. "I get possessed every day. It sucks. I'm trying to help out, but then I either sleep or a ghost decides to spend a day as me. I don't want to spend all this time with customers who don't even tip. I've spent five days here and I can't take it anymore."

Lucy watched the girl as Tamara looked away, her mouth in a firm line. She couldn't be any more than nineteen, Lucy realized. And she was exhausted.

"You're the smart one, aren't you? You've started figuring out their script. John told me that. We don't know what we'll face out there, so we really need you."

"It'll be the same the next day, and the next."

"We just have to get through today."

"We'll never clock out."

"Just...I promise, we'll figure something out." Even she wasn't sure of that vow. "This place sucks. I can see that. But we've got to survive today." If anything, only because Lucy didn't want to die. Not after...last time.

"...You just want me to do something like count change, right?" The girl with pink hair mulled it over.

"It'd help if you could bring out the coffees, too." Lucy grinned at her expression. "I mean, that spirit thought they weren't too bad, from the looks of it." Maybe she'd underestimated her coffee-making ability. She had been one of the best in her class, once her frenemy left. Deep in her heart, a brief thought flitted: There's hope.

"...Right."

Before Lucy could pry, the girl thrust a piece of paper at her and began to speak rapidly.

"They use cash and coins, exactly like we do," she said. "No cards. Fives are orange. Tens are blue. Twenties are green. Fifties are purple. There are two coins: the small, square one is a one, and the pointy, big square is a two. They don't use any cents."

"That's helpful," Lucy said.

"Not when you need to encourage someone to buy more," Tamara said. "Ninety-nine cents and everything." She leaned in, suddenly much quieter. "So, you got rid of that spirit and a monster."

"Well...sort of."

"Are you different? Like, can you do something that the others couldn't?" Her eyes narrowed. "Are you from here?"

"What? No. I'm from Earth! Always have been. Sutton, in London." She frowned. "I don't know how I could be any different from anyone here."

"If you can do something, please try and make it happen."

"We're going to gap it tomorrow." She made sure Emil was out of earshot when she said it.

Tamara looked like she genuinely appreciated that.

All of a sudden, the short girl jolted forward. Lucy caught the tiny flicker of a pale butterfly wing by her ear. On the ground below, it was a massive shadow of something amorphous with feather-like ribbons streaming out of its back. Disturbed, Lucy looked up at the wing in disbelief. When it disappeared into Tamara's ear, so did the shadow on the floor.

Tamara nearly banged her head on the counter before Lucy and John, who'd run up to them, caught her.

"Is she okay?" Lucy asked. Obviously not, but she thought she'd ask.

The girl looked up at Lucy. Blinked with big, brown eyes.
Then,
"⚥︎ℳ︎ ♎︎□︎■︎❼︎♦︎ ☟︎♏︎♏︎ℳ︎□︎♦︎ ■︎☓︎■︎ℳ︎♦︎ ♒︎ℳ︎□︎ℳ︎",
Tamara said with a wan smile.

Lucy screeched and clapped her hands over her ears. John held Tamara steady. The noise that had just come out of the girl's mouth sounded like static on a volume too high on a TV that was about to give out.

"What on Earth just happened to her?" Lucy choked out. Her ears were still ringing from whatever Tamara had said.

The girl simply smiled eerily. Before, her eyes had had a sheen to them that Lucy saw in every other person and took for granted. Now it was as though the very thing that made her human was gone.

"Emil, how does anything work over here?" Lucy could've screamed from her frustration! She looked frantically for anything else that might decide to assail them. If there were more of those things, they'd be in big trouble.

"Don't worry," John said. "It's a spirit." He looked grimly at the younger girl. "We're not likely to be possessed. The spirits kind of only choose her...I think."

Lucy scrunched her eyes shut.

"She's possessed, but we can't just leave her here. We'll take her." For a moment, Lucy wondered about the logistics of this situation, but it turned out that all the spirit in Tamara's body really did was stand there and make her look creepy. Lucy managed to sit her down in a chair. Tried dragging it—and found that it gave easily, as though Tamara was now made entirely of air.

"Huh. She's really light."

"It's a thing that happens."

With that, they placed the milk in the cart's fridge. Although John and Lucy said nothing, it was clear to each other what their plan was: If this didn't work out, they'd bolt through the city after four o'clock.

The sun was nearing its highest, and Lucy went to the entrance. "Okay, I think we're ready to go."

"Lucy."

The young woman turned to find Emil there, who was currently adjusting a glass cup full of sugar sachets, making sure they lined up with the spoons. Because that was definitely their biggest problem.

"Yeah?"

"Just so you know, I'm not giving them anything from the keyring ever."

"...Um, okay?" He sounded serious, so she didn't push it.

Instead, the young man and the woman in the beanie stepped outside with the cart in front and Tamara in tow.

Immediately, Lucy was hit with the intense cacophony of cars honking and the rush of fresh wind. Footsteps sounded in the distance. People on the balconies high above yelled and laughed. She'd actually forgotten how the entirety of the outside had sounded, being cooped up in the café for only a few hours.

"Here goes," John said, as he wheeled the cart to the threshold where the shadow of the awning met the sunny sidewalk.

Hands clammy, refusing to look at where the opening had appeared last time, Lucy nodded.

Straight-faced, they stepped over the threshold.

Nothing happened, and no trapdoor appeared on the side of the café.

Lucy let out a breath. "At least Emil was telling the truth about that. Maybe he doesn't want us to die after all?"

"Don't think for a second that he actually cares about us," John muttered.

For a moment, they looked up at the scrawled, curled signs around them, stuck to every building and every street, both feeling small.

"It's too bad Tamara's out," John said, sighing. "She'd at least be closer to cracking what they're writing if she could see it up close."

Currently, the girl was still sitting upright in the chair, smiling woodenly.

Lucy looked at the road and the street surrounding it. Even though they had to move, she was hoping to catch a glimpse of Anna, or other people she'd known who had passed. All of the people on the street at the moment were unknown to her. For the first time, Lucy felt lost.

For a brief moment, the road twisted. A sea of monsters and flickering wraiths filled the street...

She blinked. The city was normal.

Deep down, something was wrong with the memory. It didn't feel like the other things she'd seen. No pain nor emotion. This felt like she'd melded into the *city* for one split second.

She noticed that John was watching her, and she forced a smile. "Okay. Let's see where we can get some traffic." The café was tucked between two buildings, and it was practically a dead zone. People who did pass by did so without even acknowledging that they were there. Most wore business suits.

Up ahead, to their right, was a cluster of people at a giant intersection far in the distance. The two looked to each other and nodded, and John started wheeling the cart in that direction, Lucy picking up the chair and following him.

Cold and sun alternated as they walked. The towering skyscrapers cast long shadows that dipped over them, and in pockets they were suddenly free of it, and they savored the warmth. No one paid them any heed. Lucy wondered if the three of them already belonged here.

"Why did you think that we couldn't escape?" Lucy asked from behind the man.

"When we tried to run—we did manage to get out before that spirit took over—those doll hands followed us," John said darkly. "We went back of our own volition."

Briefly, Lucy thought of leaving the city. Nothing happened. She guessed that, so long as her intention was to make a profit, she could think of things such as that. Then she wondered if she could force Emil to spit out anything else he'd been keeping from them.

"Do you have a cell phone or anything?" Lucy asked suddenly.

"Never had one."

Lucy raised her brows in surprise. "Really?"

"Long story." He didn't look back. "By the way, we'll be in a really cruddy situation up there. People don't like Emil."

"He doesn't seem like he'd be popular," she offered, though the joke felt dead.

Strong light streamed through the area where they were walking, now. Lucy shaded her eyes as she dragged Tamara and turned to the source.

In a space between a lane of skyscrapers and arced buildings and high hedges and balconies was the sea, and a pier. It glistened. Waves rolled. It smelled of salt and for a moment she was back home on Earth. They weren't landlocked, it appeared, but on the coast somewhere.

Lucy's pocket began to itch with warmth. The key she still had?

"Where do you think we are?" she asked. "Because I'm stumped."

John was watching it, too. "Don't know. Do you think we could make a run for it?" Quickly, he added, "Once we've done this, I mean."

They had no idea where they'd go, but surely anywhere would be better than here.

It was burning against her skin now. She dug inside, clasped it, and it warmed against her palm instantly, nearly biting at her.

"Let's go on that side," Lucy said quickly.

The young man saw the excitement in her eyes and nodded.

Traversing the road was a mission, but eventually they got to the other side. Now the key was burning in her pocket, like a lump of hot coal, and she quickly looked around the stone pier.

Not much was there. An empty dock. A few boat sheds with oddly-shaped kayaks. A telephone booth.

The key grew hotter the closer she got to the clean glass of the telephone booth.

She turned to John. "Okay, so there's this weird thing—"

"Do what you've got to do," he said, sounding dubious.

Curiously, she stepped inside. Next to the receiver was, of all things, a keyhole. She unlocked it, and the key went cold.

The receiver picked up, and an automated message played.

"Please input how many coffees you have sold today."

The number pad was a simple layout that you could find on any telephone. Lucy punched in *1*.

"...One? Who gave you this key?"

There was static, and it was so prolonged that Lucy was about to hang up when the automated voice played again.

"Whose message do you want to listen to?"

...I guess I'll start at zero? She didn't know what she'd stumbled into. Hit the number pad.

"Message 1 of 2 from 0000. First message:"

"Uh, hi." Some young man's voice crackled onto the telephone. Lucy was sure he had an accent, with the consonants and some of the vowels sounding unlike English's, but somehow, she could understand him. "I think I'm the first one here...I woke up in this world, and I can't get back. I've found a line to record things on...um...

"...That Emil guy is suspect. He recruited me to be a barista. I had no money, so of course I decided I'd work for him. The first day was okay, but he kept telling me not to go through the back doors. He told me that this is a new city, and everyone he is going to employ has had their life taken from them."

Life taken from them?

Lucy blinked and was barely aware of the automated message playing again.

"Would you like to play Message 2 of 2 from 0000?"

Did that mean murdered? Had she been murdered?

She thought back to her last day as her heart thrummed in her throat. No, that'd been an accident, surely.

She saw John waiting, frowning now and clearly trying to hide his anxiousness, and she yanked the key out of the receiver, and it went dead. Hurriedly, she put it in her pocket and ran back out.

"Are you okay?" John asked curiously.

"The key got hot...I think I found something. I'll talk later about it." In all honesty, her head was spinning.

John said nothing as she picked up Tamara and started walking. He followed behind, and they went back into the chill cast by the skyscrapers.

Soon, Lucy's pocket was cold. She burned to listen to more of the messages, but John and Tamara were counting on her...

At the intersection, throngs of people clustered around the crossings, pedestrian and traffic lights glaring in red, blue, and pink. Dozens upon dozens of stalls were situated under the shelters and in the sun, most in an unordered line, some almost boxing people in, congesting the path. Loud and chaotic, they struggled to navigate it, let alone hear each other.

Eventually, they found a place to park, wedged between a soft drink stall and one selling children's toys.

They set up. John shouldered his way through, and Lucy went under the shelter of a shop to set Tamara in a place where she wouldn't be run over.

Her elbow collided with someone else's, and she yelped as she staggered back from a group of three women.

One spun around. Her skin was olive, and from her face she was incredibly outraged, more so than was necessary. She snapped in a high voice, "Watch where you're going!"

Her apparent abusive nature wasn't what Lucy focused on.

Short brown hair chopped messily. Olive skin. Freckles. Her lashes were short and dark. Her eyes were muddy blue. A necklace with a red rose pendant was wreathed around her neck in gold.

Amelia.

Amelia was one of the girls in Lucy's barista course. They'd been frenemies, petty, keeping with each other only because without each other they'd be lonely. Amelia had been *good* at making coffee and had left halfway through the course, which meant that Lucy had ended up in one of the higher spots. The last time they'd seen each other was the day Amelia dropped that she was leaving—and they'd gotten into an argument that Lucy had started.

But Amelia wasn't *dead.* She couldn't be.

For a brief moment, Lucy doubted herself. Yet the girl recognized her, eyes widening, and that flash of recognition, looking a little bit like a raccoon with her smudged eyeliner, was entirely Amelia's own.

"Lucy?" the girl squeaked.

"Y-You're Amelia," Lucy said quickly. "Are you...Are you really dead?"

The girl stared at her. "You're here?" she murmured. "It's you?" Her eyes flicked to John, to the coffee cart.

"You remember me?"

Amelia looked like a deer in headlights. Was about to say something. Then the girl ditched her two friends in business suits and ran.

"Amelia?" Lucy called, starting after her. Amelia could run, but so could Lucy, and the woman was taller. "Wait! I need to know—"

Five people walking in a line, taking up that part of the sidewalk, and by the time Lucy cleared them, the other woman had disappeared somewhere into the throng.

Leaving Lucy alone in a crowded intersection, the scent of pastries and petrol and soda in the air. Very, very briefly, Lucy thought of the message in the phone booth and the money, and then took a deep breath in, and started for the coffee cart, her mind whirling.

ARGUMENT

"Hardly anyone passed by us all day back at the café," Lucy said. Really, she yelled it, and she couldn't take her eyes off the swarm of colors and cars around them. This end was so crowded with people that it was difficult to focus on one person at all. "There were what, ten people?"

"The last barista said that people were avoiding us," John answered. Amongst the murmuring, the honk of car horns, and the sound of shoes hitting stone, Lucy could hardly hear him and had to lean in. "...So, what are you going to do, anyway?"

The unspoken thought that she knew was there: *How will you even sell coffee here with such busy stalls?*

Lucy took in a deep breath. Really, she wished she hadn't, because the air here was thick with cologne and petrol and all the kinds of unpleasant smells that came with being in a city. For one moment, she allowed herself to think.

Then her smile went full-wattage. "Coffee or a hot chocolate for five schmucks!" she called.

Anna had said coffees were ten schmucks. Even in a busy intersection full of food, she didn't see any hot drinks being offered. And they could compete the old way—by selling at a discount.

People looked her way immediately. *Just how good a deal is five schmucks?*

This revelation was offset when they glanced behind her, flinched, and immediately turned away.

Frowning, Lucy followed their gaze...to find John standing there, scowling, radiating dislike.

"Do you mind, er, acting happy?"

"There's nothing to be happy about," he put in seriously. "Besides, I'm here to guard you."

"We've got to act it. Otherwise, we won't get any customers."

The young man sighed and emitted a bright, fake, happy smile that looked completely at odds with his tough appearance.

"Wow. I didn't know you had that in you."

"This hurts."

67

Satisfied, Lucy turned back to the crowd and started calling again. "Coffee or a hot chocolate for five schmucks—Oh!"

A tall man had pushed his way to the front of the cart. Whereas Emil had been slightly imposing, this man was definitely so, carrying an air of gravitas like he carried the yellow jersey wrapped around his shoulders. He wore an eyepatch, which was offset by the beaded detailing of his clean, white shirt. His nose was aquiline, and his one visible, beer-brown eye was hard. In other words, he looked rich and scary.

"Have you paid for this spot?" he spat.

"...We had to pay?"

Strike one.

"How could you not realize that people pay good money to put their stalls here? Do you think this is free?" The man's eye narrowed.

"And who would *you* be?" John drawled. Lucy appreciated the backup just until the guy's face twisted like he'd just stepped on a big thorn.

"*I* am the manager of this area," the man said. "It's my job to make sure that the stalls run properly, and that they run *at a profit*." He tilted his head. "Do you want to stay here?"

"Um, yes?" Lucy said it.

"That was rhetorical. Cough up your key and don't just dawdle up here next time. Pay upfront. This spot isn't free." He outstretched his hand.

"A key?"

His one exposed eye narrowed. "You need a key to use the stall," he said, voice sounding like chipped ice.

Lucy looked at John. Begrudgingly, she handed the man the sparkly key. It felt wrong to give something like this to someone as crotchety as him, and she felt a pang as she parted with it.

"No. This thing is the wrong key." The man threw it. Lucy squeaked, but John caught it, face grim. "Surely you know what key to bring."

A very annoying memory surfaced in Lucy's mind: Emil, telling her that he wouldn't give anything up on his keyring to *them*. And she had to ask herself *why* his enemies were the people who seemed to be in control of this intersection. Did she even want to find out?

Quelling her anger, Lucy cleared her throat. "Okay...the thing is...we don't actually have a key right now."

"Oh. You don't have a *key*."

Strike two.

The man looked suspiciously at the boarded sign above their cart. In a display of total lack of care for other people's property, which by now Lucy wasn't surprised by, he pulled at the loose plank on the sign, and to their surprise, it gave way to something written in marker.

Ice seemed to grow along the pavement as his dark eye slowly drank in each swirled syllable.

"Teras Café," he said, dragging the words out. "That means you're with *Emil*." Regarding them with newfound distaste, he added, "Yet again, Emil has employed people who don't know what they're doing. And now you expect to make money without paying us?"

"We need this spot today," John argued.

"I don't care," replied the man. "Normally, if there's no key, it's fifty schmucks per hour. But for staff under Emil...two hundred and fifty per hour, and that's personal."

Emil, just how many people hate you?!

"Let us pay you a bit from what we make today," Lucy suggested quickly.

"That won't do."

"Who tattled?" John cut in, glaring at the man. "If you immediately found your way over here, just who told you?"

Next to them, the soda vendor subtly shifted his cart away a little.

"Are you going to beat our baker up?" the dark man asked, shrugging. "Because he's who alerted me. Someone unpleasant was staring at him, causing him to suffer emotional distress and making him mess up his bread. They've also been creeping out the foot traffic. I assumed it would be Emil's doing, but I decided to give you fools the benefit of the doubt."

Slowly, the two glanced over their shoulders at where Tamara had been seated. Sure enough, she was now standing up by the shiny window, behind which was a tasty array of bread, cakes, and pastries.

"...Great," Lucy muttered. She turned around to the guy and said, "If we don't make money today, we're going to die. Literally."

Strike three.

"Don't try to argue with me, because I never lose and I don't care!" snapped the man.

At the look on Lucy's face, he went on.

"I have had enough of Emil and his insane shops taking root in whatever city just so happens to be unfortunate enough to house him.

This has to stop, and I'm starting with you. I do not want a subpar stall here under my watch!"

"We can make great coffee," Lucy said. "Here, I'll prove it!"

The man waited. She hadn't thought that would work. Her fingers trembled as she went for the espresso machine.

The other stalls and some pedestrians had stopped to watch, eyes wide.

Sweat beading along her forehead, Lucy managed to make a pristine latte in record time. She placed it on the counter of the cart. "This one's free of charge," she said, laughing awkwardly, hoping her joke wasn't amiss.

Strike four.

The man looked down at it. "No."

"No?"

"No. I don't like your vibe."

"That's incredibly petty!"

"That's how I do business."

"But—!"

"How many times do I have to tell you?" the man drawled. "Get lost!"

John wedged himself into Lucy's spot behind the cart. "Take the cup. I mean it."

Scoffing, the man said, "What are you going to do about it if I don't? Move this cart immediately."

John went to sidestep the cart. Lucy saw it then—he was so tired, so sick of this that he might just punch the man. She squeaked and grabbed his arm.

The young man hesitated only for a second. It was all that Lucy had.

"Don't run at him! If you do, we'll get kicked out of everywhere in this city." Letting go of him, she said, "We'll go somewhere else." The city was teeming with people; they'd find a place to sell at eventually. "We'll take our leave."

"Good. Get out of here." Aware of John's glare, the man took the cup. "But if you insist, I'll take this to the trash myself."

"I'll get Tamara." Lucy strode over to the ghost, who stopped looking creepily through the window and instead stared at her.

"What are you doing?" Lucy hissed. "Get on the chair!"

It immediately sat down on the chair.

"Um, get out of Tamara's body?"

The ghost did no such thing.

Of course you wouldn't listen to me.

Lucy sighed, grabbed the chair, and dragged it.

Wordlessly, John began to wheel the cart away, and soon they were crossing the road.

The man watched them go, swilling the cup of coffee in his hand. The baker, an unassuming, pudgy man with stark blond hair, and the baker's assistant, who had a far less mild face, stood by him.

The baker opened his mouth. "Man, those guys were strange. They couldn't even read the script on their own sign."

His assistant said nothing, choosing to glare daggers at the three leaving, namely the dark-haired woman which was most certainly entirely reasonable. Most pedestrians had moved on, but a young woman stood by the entrance to the bakery, with dark brown hair and blue eyes, watching them go.

"Emil always employs people you'd never want," the man with the eyepatch said, sighing. "Strangers from who knows where. It's nothing new." He for a minute, then took a sip of the coffee. Then he spat it out.

"Ah, it's gross." The baker shook his head. "No wonder they were selling it so—"

"No. It's really good." The man with the yellow jersey wiped at his mouth with the back of his hand. "I was just so surprised that it took a moment for my taste buds to realize that they weren't tasting total crud."

"...You mean they're actually making *good coffee?*"

The man watched the cart, the unnecessarily violent man, and the dark-haired girl dragging another person on a chair. They weren't the weirdest sight this city had to offer, but...

"I'll have to go and get the boss," the man in the yellow jersey said. "He'll want to know about this." Wondering, he took another sip of coffee.

Amelia watched on, folding her arms to conceal her trembling.

*

At their new spot—a park—Lucy switched the cart's espresso machine on. John still glowered. Tamara looked at him and said, "⬦⬥⬦⬦ ⬦ ⬦⬦⬦ ⬦⬦⬦ ⬦⬦ ⬦⬦ ⬦⬦⬦⬦ ⬦⬦⬦⬦ ⬦ ⬦⬦⬦⬦".

"This is ridiculous," John muttered.

"What was that man's issue with us?" Lucy murmured. She tried not to think about where they were now parked. They were on the outskirts, near the pavement. Although there were plenty of people, it wouldn't have the same effect as she'd hoped.

"History, I'm guessing. And that man didn't seem like he'd be any more understanding than Emil." John looked around, and Lucy wondered if he was trying to search for their boss. To kill him? Would Emil be relaxing at a park at a time like—?

Yes, of course he would be.

Lucy cleared her throat to call their sales pitch. "Coffee or a hot chocolate for five schmucks!"

Again, a few people turned. Some walked their pets (none were dogs). Some were ambling through the gardens or watching their children. On the sidewalks, decent foot traffic. Despite her fears, there were at least a handful of people who looked interested. Still, she couldn't stop the awful, queasy feeling in her stomach.

"You okay?" John looked to her. "You've suddenly gone quiet."

Lucy hesitated, if only because this might be one of the last conversations she'd have. "I don't understand anything here," she said. "It dawned on me that I could die and I'd be a failure twice. It's on us. It's on me. This place isn't very understanding. I've seen people who I thought were dead and I might never get to talk to them."

She made herself stop before she listed all her fears, but she could feel that prickling heat on her back, her neck. It wouldn't go away.

John watched her as birds chirped. Then, finally, he shrugged. "Don't let this time we have out here be sad. You're our best shot. We don't blame you. We can't blame you. Whatever happens, we'll deal with the final tally when our job's over." He gave her a tired smile. A real one. "Don't worry about it until then. Because I'll punch a monster for you and Tamara before we go down."

Her heart still felt sick. But being free of blame for who she was—she couldn't remember the last time she'd truly felt that.

A ghost of a smile made its way onto her face. She'd had practice at that, when things were down. So she'd do it one more time. As a few people made their way over to the cart, she added, "I'm better now. I've got this. Thanks."

John nodded. "Looks like you might need help handing out coffees." He paused. "Just don't expect me to smile when I'm doing it."

PICKING UP

Lucy learned three things very quickly.

One: That there were popular tourist attractions such as a cat museum and a painting gallery (often featuring cats). Bowling was also popular here.

Two: The customers wouldn't take nines in change. In fact, they gave no currency for her to break into that amount. She'd only given out nine schmucks once as a mistake, somehow, and the woman who was waiting for her coffee paled, looked ill, and a closed, eerie ambience filled the air. The other customers had looked away, disconcerted. Lucy hadn't made that accident since.

Three: The people here needed coffee. As in, they needed it to survive.

"Of course, we all need to take a cup or two every so often," a woman in a business suit, slacks and all, was telling her. "I was surprised this was so cheap."

There was a lull in orders, so Lucy slowed down and regarded the woman anew. "Need to?"

"Everyone needs a coffee to live." Not a joke, but a recited statement, as though she'd been brought up from birth with this drilled into her. "And this is such a great blend. Actually decent coffee is rare." The woman's eyes lit up. "What's your favourite one to drink? You make them so well."

"I actually don't like coffee that much," Lucy said, laughing. "Haven't drank much of it, really."

"You don't need it?"

All of a sudden, the woman looked at her as though she had grown two heads. Then she walked away.

John looked over at Lucy from the woman, surprised. He was keeping close to the cart, guarding the money they'd made. "You alright?"

"Y-Yeah." Lucy wasn't quite sure what that information meant, so she couldn't exactly relay it. She quickly got back to work and let it slip her mind.

She learned other things, too.

People really had been avoiding their shop, which was on a main street that was usually packed. Multiple, frequent closures had made them unsure if it was even supposed to be open.

In addition, the city appeared to be on an isle. A few people mentioned boats, which confirmed that a few at least did come to port. Quietly, she added it to her mental inventory of a possible escape.

"Do you know of Emil, by the way?" Lucy asked one older man. She thought she could fish for some information, though she wasn't sure how deep her hook should be cast.

"The new business owner?" His face twisted into a suspicious scowl and his hand recoiled from the coffee. "What about him?"

"Never mind."

John returned to the cart to grab two hot chocolates off of her. "It's really picking up," he said.

"I think I've made more coffees here than I did during my entire course," Lucy said.

"They're saying it's really good. What do you put in it, anyway?"

"The hope that we'll get out of here."

John opened his mouth to say something—and then closed it. They both watched as a sleek, shining, gray car slid through the street. The windows were tinted. An emblem she'd never seen before was on the front, sparkling and golden and bisected.

"Looks flash," Lucy said. The rest resembled SUVs or sedans in subtler shades, carrying marks on them or the occasional spot of rust.

The young man watched after it quietly. What he was thinking, Lucy couldn't tell. He looked over his shoulder—and swore.

"What is she doing?"

Tamara was out of the chair, wandering around, looking up at the trees, and regarding the park. She held her brown hand out, watched the dappled light cast by the trees along her skin as she stood under them.

As if sensing their gazes, she looked at John, smirked in a way that reminded Lucy of a cat, and then took off through the park.

"I'll go get her." John darted after her.

Lucy went to say something—and then saw a line and decided to work. Surely they'd make enough. More people were gravitating towards the stall, now. A big queue was forming disturbingly quickly. It was going to take a lot of efficiency. She bit her lip and started on the next order.

*

In all honesty, John was mulling over his options. He felt lost. Punching things wouldn't solve anything?

There was the overhanging dread that they wouldn't make enough to pass, and then he'd have to fight. Because he'd seen how it ended for the other barista, got a taste of what it would be like for them.

And he was terrified.

He was sure that the answer wasn't just to go along with whatever Emil and the spirits and monsters wanted. The other way, though, was paved with violence. Staying at a café and working when they were *dead* was impossibly stupid, and he was sure that it was Emil's sick idea of a joke to toy with them before he inevitably got them killed.

He wanted to get back at their boss—today. He didn't know if that'd be possible.

The ghost possessing Tamara took a hard left, towards the rose garden and some trees bearing blue fruit that looked a bit like olives.

John ran up to her—and found that the ghost was touching the tree in curiosity.

"Oi. What are you doing?" John asked. "Get out of her body."

If anything, the ghost seemed to be enamored with the sun, the dappled light, and the tree bark. Okay, that was good—

It used her fingers and sharp nails (John noted that they must have cost a bomb at whatever salon she went to in her previous life and wondered how she'd react when she saw them ruined) and tore off some bark.

Then it went to pop it in her mouth.

"Woah, woah." John plucked it from the girl. "You can't make her eat that! What are you thinking?"

The ghost considered this. Then it pointed to the plastic playground in the distance and stared at John.

"No. You are *not* going over there. What are you, five?"

"⚸♋■⋈♏● ⋈⋆ ⋆□♏♋⚷⋈■♈". It turned around and started for the roses. Made Tamara crouch down and smell them. At the subtle scent, it scowled and rubbed at her nose.

"...Tch. You've never been outside, have you? Is it always you who jumps into the body? Or are there all sorts of different spirits possessing her?"

He stopped as he realized that passersby in the park were watching him, clearly regarding him as problematic and weird. Never mind that Tamara was now pulling a few out of the tidy garden and was starting to make a rose daisy chain.

Right. The people here didn't actually seem to be cognizant of monsters until one was EATING them.

Embarrassment aside, he stood by Tamara as the ghost busied itself with the roses. Watched over her.

They'd arrived in the café together, the two of them. Both had woken up, and he'd seen the slight girl with pink hair who must have been even younger than him. They'd stared at each other.

"Did you die?" she'd asked.

For a moment, he was surprised. He hadn't expected that question; he'd thought that was a dream.

"...Yeah," he'd said. His voice was parched. "I died."

The girl had held no sympathy. She'd just nodded quietly, drawn her legs towards her chin, and rested there. It'd taken him a while to get her to help him.

They'd tested all the darkened windows. The door was locked and didn't break no matter what he threw at it. They didn't understand it, and John could see the city beyond the windows, and he knew that it was completely different than Earth. They'd both known it.

"It's not a script anywhere in the world," the girl had said.

He'd frowned at her.

She'd pointed outside. "The writing on the signs is something I don't recognize. I don't think we're...anywhere we should be."

It'd felt odd having his thoughts confirmed just like that.

She'd noted the newspaper, flicked through it, and dully sat down on a standing chair. Two strands of her cotton-candy-pink hair fell forward. She'd looked like she was going to go to sleep.

He checked every possible exit. It was still dark outside. Then John had given up, and he'd rested his back on the frame of the door. He'd wanted to ask, *What do you think is going to happen to us?*

Suddenly, they'd heard it. A banging out back.

Pushing himself off the frame, John went to cross the empty counter. It was layered with streaks of dust.

"Don't," the girl had said quickly. He turned to find her with her big brown eyes suddenly a lot sharper. In them, he saw confusion just as intense as his own.

It was then that he'd decided he could trust her.

"That's such a bad idea," she had added, and her tone turned harsh. She'd hugged herself. "Don't you know what happens in horror movies? People go and investigate a noise, and they die."

"Help me!" called a voice. It had sounded like another guy. Not quite panicked, but...sharp.

John had pointed to the door. "I've got to go and see what's behind here. You know that, right?"

"Well, don't expect me to go over there and help you!" The girl had looked away and stared at the windows. The neon lights outside hadn't reflected in her eyes.

John had watched her. As he did, the dark switched to day. The first word that came to John's mind: alien. A thought that this was some strange place in the middle of nowhere.

He'd weighed it up in his mind. They were trapped here, and she was scared, no matter how composed she was. And the only way was to move forward. So he turned and left for the weighted doors.

Was that her fear he'd felt when he opened them?

He'd regretted going *out back,* of course. He'd regretted that whole day. The whole situation was messed up.

He'd try to keep Tamara—and now Lucy—safe. He just wished he could make Emil answer for something, anything. If they were going to die, they could at least have a punch-up where John *won.*

"Guess I can't do that today," he murmured. Right now, the key he had was useless. They had to get to morning, but...

His eyes felt tired against the harsh blue of the sky.

Eventually, the ghost in Tamara's body grew bored, picked a few petals off the roses, chucked them away, and then stared at him.

"If you're bored, let's go back." He gave her his hand.

The ghost, curious, took it and laughed. It tried to pull him towards the playground.

He didn't have time for this.

John helped the possessed girl up, and then they made their way back. The people around them still thought they were mildly strange.

When they got to the edge of the park, John found that Lucy and the coffee cart were inundated. The young woman and her beanie were barely visible amongst the throng of people.

Holy...her coffee's that good?!

The other barista had *also* made decent coffee. This was on an entirely different level.

Lucy's eyes found his. She took in a deep breath. "Um, I need some help."

"Shoot." John placed Tamara back in her seat. "I've got you."

They got to work, and soon he was dealing out coffee to patient customers. Things were looking up.

Until they weren't. All of a sudden, a car screeched onto the pavement, its tires parked on the curb. It was the same sleek car that had sped by earlier.

People recognized it and slowly backed away. Lucy and John looked to one another.

The door swung open with one fluid motion. Out stepped a man in a blue, cashmere turtleneck. His face was stern. His right ear was pierced with black. He wore expensive-looking shoes that shone with incredible intensity. His hair was meticulously cropped and chestnut. Fierce green eyes gazed at the coffee cart, and his sunglasses, perched on top of his head, were an expensive brand whose rims looked like they could slice through diamonds.

Emil watched and tsked as he ate a sandwich from the shop across the road. The narration was hovering on this guy, too. He'd never seen a description that intense. No one that important ever attended the café.

Which meant that, for some reason, the girl in the beanie was important after all.

AMBULANCE

The businessman surveyed the scene before him. Someone was operating an unauthorized coffee cart out here. It wasn't quite the loss of profit that he was angry about, although that was serious business (Montgomery remembered the exploding coffee incident), and in this city, business was everything. So was keeping people alive. Thus, it was with annoyance and mild trepidation that he regarded the special coffee cart and the dozens of people crowding it.

Three workers were manning the stall, though one seemed more intent on looking at the sun. He'd never seen them in the city before.

More of them?

Not that it mattered, he supposed. The coffee cart would have to be removed and destroyed.

Lucy didn't know who this man was, of course, so when he arrived at the cart—everyone around them was suspiciously silent, unwilling to look the man's way—she ended up staring, not really being able to say anything at all. Clearly, he was a big deal.

"And what..." He pointed to the words at the top of the cart. "...is this?"

John muttered, "Not again."

Lucy cleared her throat. "We're selling coffees and hot chocolates out here today. We can offer you...a free one?" Hey, she'd try it. Though he didn't seem like he needed free *anything*.

"Do you know what you're doing here?" the man asked.

Lucy was sure this would lead to this man telling them to get lost, which seemed inevitable at this point. She couldn't fathom losing the cluster of people who were still hanging around, prepared to ask for coffee, and she mentally skipped the conversation and started thinking of how to argue her point.

So it was to her surprise when he opened his mouth at her non-answer and said, "Did you die before?"

John, who was still beside her, had eyes like pinpricks as he regarded the man. The other pedestrians merely milled, talking amongst themselves, seemingly too afraid to listen in.

Unlike all of them, this man seemed to have a clue about what was going on.

Lucy found herself not knowing what to say. "I"—She noted the badge along his lapel, a gold, embossed cup of coffee. The look on his face—he must have been in his early thirties—didn't particularly strike her as *nice*. So she faltered. "...I...It's my first day in the city."

The man considered this. Then he slightly rolled up his left sleeve.

His hand and wrist were deeply scarred. Purple, with chewed-up skin.

Those are the marks of an animal tearing at someone. Lucy knew it just from sight.

"Yes or no. Did you die before?"

"...Yes. How do you know about us?"

"I'm the head of the Café Union. We can't have anyone who's not in the Union selling drinks out here."

"Why not?" Lucy asked as John said, "Did they really nark on us?"

"Apparently, you were causing quite the commotion downtown. I don't know if I approve of coffee being sold here for cheap, either. It's important. We don't really like competitive prices."

"It's just for today. It's a special—"

"Cut it out," John said, suddenly walking out from behind the cart. "What's the real reason? Is it because you know we're not from here?"

"Since it's likely your last day, I'll tell you," the man said. Lucy realized with a hole in her stomach that the man wasn't there to help them. "We need the cart."

"You're not having it," John said, waving him away.

"Yeah, we really can't give you the cart. It's...not for sale," Lucy said.

"Do you know why you're working?" the man asked.

"More or less."

"Do you know why you're here?"

At this, John tensed, and Lucy realized that neither of them wanted to answer. Did he know, too? *We had our lives taken from us. Somehow, that's why we're here.*

Which would lead to more questions.

No. They couldn't be out here discussing things like this. There couldn't be doubt between them today. She killed the conversation.

"I'm sorry, but you simply can't have this cart." It was surprisingly easy how she said it.

"Oh, I mean that I'm towing it."

"What?"

A truck rolled into view. Four buff men hopped out, all in a branded brown uniform.

Lucy squeaked as John cursed and rounded on the man. "You can't do that!"

"I'm the head of the Café Union," the man said, waving them away. "What I say goes. And I want this cart towed and gone."

"All our money is here!" Lucy's voice cracked when the guy simply walked away. She spun to John and said, "You need to chain yourself to the cart, stat!"

"What?"

Lucy *had* been kicked out of university for her strange ideas.

Seeing that John was not obliging this very reasonable request, Lucy quickly dove for the register. It popped open.

Heaps of fives and tens and some twenties. Coins. There was one big problem.

"The cash machine is stuck to the cart. I don't think we'll be able to move this change without losing a few." *And lose our way of making money!* "Don't come any closer!"

The four men advanced.

John was immediately in front of Lucy, cracking his knuckles. "Emil told me that I had to protect the furniture at any cost," he said to her.

"Not questioning it."

He struck out with surprising speed and slammed his fist into one guy's temple. Lucy was *not* sure how legal all of this was, but she wasn't going to start questioning how he went about bodyguarding when their lives were on the line.

It was impressive, really. Maybe he was outclassed by literal monsters, but this guy could *fight,* and he fought dirty.

Two men engaged him. The other two simply walked around the fight and went for the coffee cart.

Shoot.

"Don't take it away," Lucy said, panicking as one of the men in uniform approached the cart.

This one was a little different—he was bald, with gray eyes. He seemed to be in charge of the operation. "Move aside," he said. "Montgomery wants it gone."

John was doing fabulously against the men, but he was tired. Wouldn't last long. Lucy watched John kick one of the workers in the shin. They were still upright—in pain, but upright—and he was slowing down.

Lucy began to sweat as an idea came to her.

She'd felt an overwhelming emotion when the generator had kicked into gear back in the café: the need to hide away. The exact same flux she felt when she'd approached the other monsters. Did that mean that something was blocking a monster?

Was there a monster *inside* the coffee cart? She was sure of it.

Her brows raised. *The generator. It must be stuck behind there.*

For a moment, she thought that she could run, pull the wire out, and set it loose. Knowing the monster's viciousness and the intensity of the feeling of antisociality, though...Whoever pulled that out would have to be one of the men trying to tow it. They were close, now.

"Please don't take it!" Lucy tried again, shielding it, wondering if she could pull this off.

As the bald man sidestepped her, he hooked up an extremely long cable to the cart. Lucy blurted out, "The generator! At least let us keep the generator. You just want the coffee cart, right?"

The man glared at her—and then shrugged. "Take the generator out before I move it," he told his lackey. Then he turned and called sharply, "Hey! He'll need some help."

By now, John was restrained. A man with cropped hair held him as another jogged up to where Lucy stood. John went to bite his remaining captor's arm, and the man slapped him. Lucy drew in a sharp breath.

Okay, now I don't feel bad at all.

The bald man left, and two others pulled at the generator. That stubborn wire came undone from its lock.

Out popped a snakelike creature as the wire crashed to the ground. Black-green scales undulated, heavy fangs dripped, and tiny, flabby wings, alongside tiny decorations that looked to be baubles on its extremely large body, twitched.

And all hell broke loose.

The bystanders screamed. The man who still held the generator shrieked as it launched for his face. The other guy managed to haul it off, but it rounded back fast as lightning and bit him in his—

Redacted!

At the end of this exciting slaughter, two men were face down. John's restrainer was now severely injured by a wayward fang, and the bald man was now keeping the vicious monster back with a stick. Somehow, the truck had been smashed. There were no casualties amongst the bystanders, who stood back and didn't move and looked horrified. John was now creeping towards Lucy, who was standing behind the coffee cart and trying to hide, immensely proud, and extremely terrified.

Tamara was out of her chair, and Lucy found the girl standing beside her, flat eyes gleaming like a cat that was incredibly pleased with her. As though Lucy had just done something on purpose.

"Why can't we have a day without a freaking accident?" the man in charge of the operation yelled in despair, bringing her back to the present. Strange; he was bald, but they were clearly kindred souls.

"Good thinking," John hissed, sidling over to Lucy, watching the onslaught. "...How are we going to get it back in there, though?"

She took in a breath. Had an idea that was based entirely on luck, but it was their only option.

As if sensing this question—and Lucy's decision—the snake-monster turned to Lucy and began to slither her way. It looked like it was deciding on whether to bite her or not, and it was entirely too reminiscent of the lizard-like one's encounter, and she knew she had to speak up.

Clearing her throat, she said, "We want to hook the generator back up. Those guys took it out when I told them not to." *I'm already lying to a monster that can figuratively kick my butt.* She scrambled to the generator. "John, help me out!"

"On it."

They hefted it, and Lucy noticed that the snake-monster seemed to be scowling as they fumbled with the wires. She wanted to tell it that they were trying, but she guessed that'd just make it even angrier. Eventually, though, John went to put the last wire in. The monster hopped up (could snakes hop? Lucy found out today that yes, this one could) and wriggled into the tiny hole.

As it passed, she felt a brush of emotion. The feather of a man locking his apartment door, shutting out the world. She was reminded of the dog-monster attached to the fridge, and something prickled at the back of her mind. That monster was attached to a space that could count as furniture, too...

Though she didn't know what that *meant.*

John quickly put the wire back in, grimacing.

Silence ensued. The birds in the park chirped.

The two surviving men supported one another. Lucy coughed, now not really feeling all that great about siccing the monster on them, but it was too late. She didn't miss how John didn't even bat an eye and how the ghost seemed very pleased.

"You've done something you'll regret," the bald man said. His voice was low. "You can't just harm members of the Café Union."

"If you've got a problem with how we run business, take it up with Emil," John said, shrugging. "He's the man you want. We're just doing our jobs."

The bald man glared at them. He was bleeding profusely. The bystanders in the park, oddly enough, were all still there. Apparently, a fight to the death with a monster hadn't just happened. Or it wasn't enough to freak out over. Either way, they were unperturbed.

"You might want to get an ambulance," Lucy offered. "I can call—"

The man frowned. "What the heck is an ambulance?"

They limped off, choosing to use another car instead of the totaled truck.

After a beat, the would-be customers gathered back at the coffee cart. Their faces were smooth and their orders were normal. Against their chatter and the smell of coffee, the birdsong in the park sounded exactly like that on Earth.

This place is so freaking strange, Lucy thought.

They sold coffee for the rest of the afternoon.

And with that, Emil's business was dragged into everything that followed.

RESULT

They arrived back at the café at ten to four. The sky was still bright and sunny, but John had told her that they needed to put the cash in the till before the shop closed. He'd looked kind of ill when he'd said it and had offered no other explanation.

It seemed as though the city was winding down. After three, the number of customers at the park had started thinning. Fewer people walked the streets on their way back. She could actually hear herself think at the intersections. In the distance, the harbor sparkled. When they'd passed it again, there were still no boats.

Under the awning, Affogato sat by the entrance. Its big green eyes fell on Lucy. Then, as if it'd been waiting for them, it turned and squeezed through the tiny gap in the door, apparently satisfied. The bell jingled.

Lucy toyed with the cuff of her uniform's sleeve. *We had less time than normal,* she told herself. They were almost out of milk, anyway, and they'd stocked the bulky fridge to the brim with coffee, chocolate powder, and cartons. Her bitten hand was sore.

There were so many excuses.

She'd done the best she could, despite how crazy this place was. That often wasn't enough. But today...perhaps it was enough for her to hold her own.

When they stopped at the awning, she smelt sweet pastries across the road, saw how verdant all the hedges along those strange balconies were, and found herself wishing that she could stay here. If not go back home, stay here and stay alive.

"I've never seen someone move that fast when they're fighting, by the way," Lucy said, because she didn't want their last words to be something work-related. "Just thought I'd put it out there."

A wry smile. "Practice." Maybe he knew not to talk about the café, too, because he let the subject drop.

They looked at each other, nodded, and took a step under the awning.

As they passed under the canopy, Tamara jolted in her chair and suddenly became the actual weight of a person again. Lucy, juggling the new weight and careful not to let her just drop, twisted to see a large shadow flitting out along the pavement, darting into the shop.

The two watched as Tamara swayed. Her long lashes fluttered. She looked around, noticed that she was sitting on a chair and that they were outside, and said, glancing down, "It's that time, isn't it?"

"Well—"

The girl sighed. "Never mind. I don't want to know. I guess it doesn't matter." She didn't make a move to walk towards the door—not that Lucy didn't blame her—so she helped her up.

"We did our best. We might make it," Lucy said.

"We actually might," John added from ahead. Already, the coffee cart was ticking towards the door.

"Tomorrow's booked out, too?" Tamara felt heavy.

"You did well," John said. Whether he was talking to Lucy or Tamara or both, it wasn't clear. It didn't really matter.

They stepped inside.

*

The café was empty. Music still played.

Between John and Lucy, the two transferred the money into the till under the front counter. While they did so, a conflicted thought flitted through Lucy's mind.

As much as I hate this place, I've never felt more alive than today. Somewhere in there, amongst all that chaos, she got the chance to actually be a barista rather than perpetually training for it. She practically ran everything with zero help from her boss, if only for a couple of hours. She got a taste of what it could be. And fought a couple of monsters and won, too. That was...

She wasn't grateful, not really, but if there *was* something to be grateful for, that was it.

The till locked tight.

John handed her the mop. Wordlessly, she took it, noting that he'd retrieved the steak knife. Then he went to stand by Tamara, who was staring at the counter, the impervious wall. Lucy took Tamara's other side.

One minute after four, and abruptly the café fell into darkness. Lucy turned to see stars clustered in swirls, twinkling outside, brighter than any she'd ever seen on Earth. Signs flickered neon. With the high rises that boxed the street in, vast shadow swathed the pavement and the awning.

Howls and wails rose from behind the doors. The chandelier and the other lights above them cut out.

Lucy swallowed thickly. Tamara quickly took a step back, eyes big. John's lips were pressed together tightly, and he stared straight ahead.

Emil strode in, the bell jingling as he did so, carrying the scent of smoke inside. He made no move to lock the door. Sunglasses were still perched on his Roman nose despite the overwhelming darkness. He rounded past them.

If you're going to die, at least speak up! Lucy cleared her throat. "Where were you?" she asked.

"You were busy, weren't you? So I didn't interfere." Emil made no other comment and instead went to the cash register and started cashing up.

Flick. Flick. Flick. The man in red leafed through the paper and metal expertly. No one said a word. Lucy looked to the door behind him, the one that led to the hallways, and her palms laced with sweat as she noticed eyes, dozens of them, a thousand more unseen, almost indistinguishable in the dark, watching them.

Emil stopped counting. "You sold our coffee rather cheaply," he said, writing something in a checkbook.

"Well."

He tapped a calculator. Then he put the money in plastic bags.

"This is enough to keep the pop-up café running for another day."

The howls and wails thrummed through the floorboards...and then the presences behind the door vanished abruptly. Eyes gone. Two normal doors. A small light on the ceiling flicked on.

Emil stood up and looked at them. "Congratulations."

"Wait. So we made it out alive?" Tamara asked. She sounded dubious. Lucy couldn't quite believe it, either.

"For today, yes."

A moment of silence—and then Lucy let out a small breath of relief. Then she choked as she was locked into a hug by the other two beside her.

"Oh my gosh, we get to live!" Tamara squealed, sounding very much not like herself.

"You did it, Lucy!" John cried. He hauled her up and she yelled as her beaten shoe broke off completely.

Out there at the back of the café, Lucy knew there were monsters. Multitudes of them, all wishing they'd failed.

They could be disappointed.

"I'm still docking your pay for the lunch you didn't have," Emil called. "You're supposed to take it."

It doesn't matter, she thought as Tamara screeched and Emil told her to knock it off. *You actually...did it.*

*

Lucy's mind was full of questions when she was on solid ground again, once the excitement had died down and she'd scarpered to the counter and grabbed her coat and old clothes. *I'm never leaving these out of my sight again. Can I get my beanie mended?*

Emil slugged his jacket over his shoulder. "Well, it's night," he said, pointing out the obvious. "I guess I should give you your keys."

All were silent. Lucy was the last to receive hers—cold and light, small in her palm. A plain, gold key with a butterfly-shaped ward.

"It's for an apartment," Emil said.

Relief and thankfulness flitted through her. Apparently, this wasn't where she would be sleeping.

Tamara was already out the door. John grabbed their map that'd been taped to the bottom of a table. The coffee cart rested behind the counter.

"Where did all the monsters go?" Lucy asked her boss.

"Second story," Emil said.

"Do we have to w—"

"I need to close up the shop and go home. I'm not letting you make me stay overtime." He grabbed a cigarette.

Was she being passed up for a smoke break?

Yes, she was. He went outside, glared at her from behind his shades and the window, and took a drag.

Sighing, Lucy walked outside. The air was crisper, smoother. Tamara stood waiting for her. Cars still sped past and what people were left still walked briskly, but many shops were already shut. The city went to sleep early, apparently. The pavement was cold against her sock.

"You've got to tell me what happened with my nails," Tamara said grimly, holding up her ruined, ruby-red gel attachments. That dampened mood was back on.

"Um, I think you've got to ask John about it. The spirit...ghost...did a runner."

She looked up to the high-rises above. "I hate being possessed."

John trudged out—and walked right past them, onto the neon-soaked part of the sidewalk. A sign displaying a winking tiger was lit up in pink. Its eye kept winking at them.

"Hey." Lucy started after him. "Don't we need to figure out what we're going to do?"

He looked back at them. "We'll have to end up here again, anyway. We'll try the key tomorrow morning. Seven."

"You don't want to get something to eat?"

"I've got something to do."

Without another word, he strode along the pavement, blending in with the ambling crowd.

He'd said it quite coldly. Why blow them off now, after the terror that was the café? That was...completely at odds with what he was like during work.

Watching Lucy, Tamara said, "It looks like most of the shops are closing. *I* am starving, by the way."

"How do we know where our apartment is? And food."

"Emil said it was back that way when you were getting your stuff." Tamara nodded at...the direction Lucy had woken up in. The side street. Now that it was night, a good portion of people were in that direction, all heading home.

"I hope I can get there without getting glass in my foot. My shoe has had it. I guess that's what I'm spending my paycheck on."

Tamara snorted, but she didn't smile. Hadn't since that brief moment in the café. Instead, she looked...impassive. Her face was very smooth and her eyes were distant.

Abruptly, Tamara's expression changed to disgust as she looked to the café windows and scowled. "Ugh, it's watching us."

Lucy glanced back and saw Affogato perched underneath one of the chairs, green eyes glowing.

"It's kinda cute." She owed it her life, after all.

"The cats here creep me out." Tamara shrugged, though Lucy wondered how much Tamara really didn't care. "Notice anything about the clothes in this place?"

Lucy shaded her eyes against the glare of the halogens. Looked at the shop across the road. "They're all...work uniforms. No way."

"There are some nicer ones near the back."

"Don't these people have anything better to do in the afterlife?"

"It might not *be* the afterlife."

"Emil—"

"Never confirmed it to me or John."

Another headache that would have to marinate before Lucy could even attempt to grasp the concept with some clarity of thought.

Tamara glanced over her shoulder. "I think we're going the same way. Same kind of key, yeah?"

Wait...have Tamara and John been locked in there this whole time? What kind of boss is Emil?

Speaking of whom, he'd gone back into the café. It was shut, now. As if any of them would even want to step right back in there.

Remembering the phone booth and the blue key in her pocket, Lucy made herself stop from taking the invite. "I've got something I have to do. Want to come along?"

Tamara tilted her head. "I'll see you around. I think food and an actual bed are that way." She hiked her thumb back at the side street in the distance.

*

Lucy arrived at the telephone booth and snuck inside through the dark glass door. It was possible that it wouldn't work in the morning, that it reset every day, so she couldn't chance it. As she assumed it would, it asked her the same question as before: *How many coffees have you sold today?*

She'd actually kept track, marked it on Tamara's scrap of paper with the money values, determined to get here and work things out.

"Whose message would you like to listen to?"

She pressed *0*.

The message that played first was the same. Emil wasn't to be trusted. Listening to it a second time, Lucy realised that this young man's experience was somewhat different from hers. The city was *new*. So he might have been the very first of them. She pressed the receiver closer to her ear as he spoke the last sentence.

"Everyone he is going to employ has had their life taken from them."

"Would you like to play Message 2 of 2 from 0000?"

"Yes," Lucy said quietly. She went to punch in a number, but it must have heard her. The second message began playing. His voice was less hurried. More confident.

"I've been here a while, now. People need coffee here to live. You need to trust your coworkers. They're the only ones in the same boat as you. Three of them ended up here the second week I was working."

Lucy toyed with the phone wire.

"We discovered something about the dead people from our past. The ones who remember you are the ones who are important."

Lucy blinked.

"That's all."

The message cut off. His final entry? That was it?

Skin prickling, Lucy went to try another message from another worker, but sharp rapping on the glass made her look to her left. Someone was out there, motioning for her to get away. They were small, and she couldn't make out who they were with shadows falling on the booth, but it looked like they were panicking.

Quickly taking back the key and pocketing it, Lucy walked outside. When she did, she found that Anna was standing there in the gloom. It looked like her face was beaded with sweat, though she wasn't out of breath.

"An—Hey," Lucy said. "Is there a problem?"

"A cat's on the prowl," Anna said, as if that answered everything. "If it sits on the phone booth, it'll be out of operation until it decides to get up and move on."

Those words strung together in that way gave her an immediate headache. Very confused, Lucy looked around and saw a white cat sniffing around the parking lot nearby. It promptly jumped on a car that'd been starting to reverse. The engine died immediately. The young man who was going to drive it got out, tipped his hat slightly to the curled-up beast, and then he made his way on foot.

Lucy snorted a laugh. Seriously, what was this place?

Anna squeaked and took her by the arm.

The cat had heard the woman's giggle, too. Its ears twitched, and it turned to look at her with big, blue eyes.

Its aura of cold judgement and indifference seeped forward. Lucy's skin skittered. This was nothing like the look the sweet black-and-white cat back in the café had given her. A cat deciding to situate itself on a car was, apparently, serious business.

The cat continued to stare at her. Shoot, did it think she was challenging it?

"Don't giggle at a cat," Anna whispered. "It hurts their pride. Oh my gosh, and don't stare at it! What are you doing? Do you want to die?"

"No," Lucy hissed, kind of panicked.

"If you move back slowly, and we go towards the harbor, it should leave you alone. Lower your eyes."

Gulping, Lucy did as the girl suggested. Eventually, they got to the edge of the port. Lucy guessed that the cat had gone back to sleep, since she no longer felt like something wanted to swipe her face.

They sat on a stone bench, waves lapping below.

"Thanks," she said quietly.

"No problem." Anna bit into a pastry, which looked really good right about now. Lucy's stomach was in knots. "If a cat sits on anything, you can't use it. And they get feisty if you don't pay the proper respects."

"Like back where I'm from," Lucy said, giving a little laugh. Quietly, though, so the cat didn't hear her. "If they've got cats here, where are the dogs?"

"Hmmm. We don't see them that often."

Get me out of here. "Guess I don't know all there is to know about felines. Seriously, thanks." A thought flitted through her mind. Did Anna remember her? Which would mean she was important, somehow. That would save her so much time—

"I thought I'd save the woman who actually gave me a coffee I could scarf down. You looked lost, so I kinda felt sorry for you."

She doesn't remember me. "I'm still getting used to the city. It's making my head spin."

"First day?"

"Something like that." Seeking to change the topic, Lucy perked up as she saw some artwork along the harbor shops' windows.

They were admittedly garish, with bright pops of pink, scarlet red, ultramarine, and an extremely bright, almost brownish yellow. The Anna she knew would've probably been all over them.

"Those look cool." Lucy nodded to the shop. "You were checking out the paintings in the café, right? Do you ever think of trying out painting yourself?"

"I do sometimes."

"You should, like, display them or something. And sell them." Remembering the small canvases, the sheets of paper Anna used to hide from everyone and show only her, keeping their dreams between themselves, as though anyone else catching wind of them would cause them to break...At least that part hadn't changed.

Anna searched her face hard.

"You know, when I look at you...you do kind of remind me of home. Even though home's here." The girl frowned. "It's not a feeling I'm used to. Don't tell anyone I said that, though."

Lucy breathed in.

So. So she *is* from Earth, Lucy thought. And she had her own life here. That...was enough for her. She could handle her not really knowing her, just so long as she knew she'd be alright.

It also dawned on her that Amelia had recognised her. Which meant confronting her.

"I've just got one of those faces, I guess."

The girl turned away from her, dropping pastry crumbs. Her expression was suddenly very, very serious. "I'm also here to ask you something."

"Yeah?"

A tilt of the head.

"I heard you were selling your coffee out there for five schmucks. I gave you ten. Where's my change?"

Lucy broke into a grin. Couldn't help it. Yeah, that was Anna.

"It's a long story. If you go to the café again, I'll give you a free one."

"Your boss didn't tell you what to charge, did they? You're blooming lucky I turned around and gave you money. What kind of boss is that, anyway...?"

APARTMENT

By the time Lucy got to the apartment complex—a towering building with intricate, coiling gold molding along its front, a wide, shining set of sliding doors, and far too many hedges on overhangs from the fifth story upwards—she was exhausted. Her foot ached. Her coat was hanging from her shoulders, now, and all she wanted was a nice bed to lay her head down on.

The simple key, unlike the other one, hadn't warmed up when she'd gotten close to the doors. Instead, she'd simply asked a car salesman down the road where the apartments were. Saved her a lot of time.

"Useless key," she muttered, yawning as the glass slid open.

A warm reception area, with aircon rattling. Lucy was about to consider that the café needed that, too, but she tossed that thought away with the determination to focus on anything else except her workplace.

People lounged in the waiting area, reading books or quietly playing chess. An empty counter had a large bell. She thought she saw movement behind the glass in what must have been reception's office.

There was a vending machine amongst the lounging chairs, displaying seven rows of plastic packaging. Lucy's mouth watered, and she rummaged through her pockets—and then remembered she didn't have any money.

Never mind.

Bypassing all of that, Lucy went straight to the elevator. There was a keyhole, which she plugged her new key into, and the cabin's lights started blipping as it moved upwards.

What floor she was on, she had no idea. Just that it was *high*.

It was nothing compared to some of the skyscrapers here, of course, and from the view in the hallway, it seemed they were wedged between the view of a purple building's walls (some people were still in the office doing their paperwork. Lucy wished they'd pull their blinds down) and the roof of a gray, stone, vertical carpark. On the tips of her toes, though, she could see a black, winding street that seemed to go on forever. She couldn't even see another view of the ocean from way up here.

Nope. Not thinking about how this city might go on forever.

Yawning, she went to find her room.

After a few tentative tries and awkward conversations, she found her room. She tried to memorize the symbol she couldn't read. The door wouldn't open; there was no keyhole.

"Useless key," she cried.

Someone noticed her struggling and showed her how to open it—one tap on the metal door with the key, and it unlocked. Wanting to cry, she thanked them, barreled inside, and collapsed on the entranceway floor, stopping the door from being able to close.

Over her wafted the smell of clean sheets, stale petrol through an open window, and packaged dish soap. Heaven.

"Wow. Day one did a number on you. Don't die on us here."

Cracking open an eye, Lucy found Tamara. The door opposite hers in the hallway was open, revealing a white-and-brown room just like Lucy's, the mirror image. Tamara had changed clothes—a shirt with a contrast collar, shorts. Must've been her old ones she teleported in.

Revived. Whatever.

"I'm going to go to sleep here," Lucy said.

The girl raised an arched brow. "I've got snacks."

Lucy stood up. "If you have food, come in."

Soon, they sat on plush chairs in Lucy's apartment. Biscuits (these tasted bitter, like matcha). A sandwich (ham. Maybe). A bottle of orange juice.

"How did you get these?"

"It's a secret."

"Nah, you've got to tell."

"What would you do if I told you that Emil gave John and me food cards? They work on the vending machine down there."

Lucy closed her eyes. "I'm going to steal his stupid sunglasses and make sure he never finds them again." *Trying* not *to think of all the ways he's wronged me today.*

Tamara broke off a piece of her sandwich and looked out the window. "...Thanks. For saving us." For a brief moment, she sounded wistful.

They fell into awkward silence. Well, Lucy did, anyway. Tamara looked like she was comfortable with not speaking. In fact, it seemed like there was a whole conversation she was having in her head. Was she writing a novel in there? Lucy needed *noise*.

"John said you were from Spain."

At that, Tamara *almost* smiled. "Best beaches, best mountains, best food. Would it surprise you if I said that my parents were party planners?"

"Both of them?"

"Mhm. They held the best ones. My aunt, too. That's why they were so in demand. We went everywhere with them." Something flickered in her eyes. Mouth straight, she said, "I wonder if anyone here ever does that."

Neon flickered along her face and the table. Lucy's view was smack-bang against the purple building. On the street below, she noted how the buildings were constructed. Shops were stacked on top of other shops, turrets of mismatched colors, architecture, and wares. If it weren't for all the greenery unifying it, it'd probably give her a headache.

"Apparently, there's a bowling alley. Not quite partying, but it's something to do. I'd like to go on my day off."

The street below blurred before her eyes, and Lucy looked up. Although the purple building that took up most of the window was high, she could still see those pinpricks of white, all in foreign constellations.

"I knew this city was full of total squares," Tamara said blandly.

Her voice seemed far away. Lucy wondered what the rest of this world looked like.

*

Tamara stayed in Lucy's apartment for what seemed like hours. They were the only normal people from Earth here, really, so Lucy didn't mind. Neither seemed to want to speak about today—or even tomorrow, so they kept themselves busy by people-watching the street below. The food was all gone (apparently, there was a limit to the vending machine, six items a day). It must've been...

Only nine o'clock.

"Oooh, look at him," Lucy exclaimed, leaning forward in her chair.

A thief in a thick purple coat pocketed his wire cutters and took off on a parked bike. Started to speed up under the cover of night—

An orange cat jumped onto the seat out of an alleyway. The thief skidded to a halt, nearly dropped the bike, hurriedly fumbled with it into an upright position when he saw the cat, stood it against a

97

lamppost with the cat balancing on it perfectly, tipped his hat, and went away on foot. He was then tackled by a man who Lucy assumed was security.

One side of Tamara's lips turned up just slightly. "Okay, that was *almost* funny."

The office building's lights were almost all out, now. One young man—an office junior, probably—was still stuck inside doing his paperwork at a long computer. Lucy felt incredibly sorry for him.

She went to say something—and then a tail brushed against her leg. She giggled, looked down, and saw Affogato there, staring up at her.

She beamed.

"Hey, little guy. How'd you get out of the café? Did Emil finally decide to let you go?" He must've snuck in through the gap under the door.

A sharp grating of the chair beside her. She turned to see Tamara standing up, her face suddenly gray.

"What's—?"

"That thing's following you?" The girl's brown eyes tracked it, and she took another step back.

"Oh, yeah...Funny story, he actually helped me when—"

In fifteen quick steps, Tamara was out the door. In twenty, she'd reached her room. Her door shut almost instantaneously.

Lucy got up to go and check on her, but she heard the click of a lock. Two locks, actually.

In the middle of the apartment now, she turned to look at Affogato, who stared back, unbothered. Her own door clicked shut.

Frowning, Lucy crouched down and scratched it, felt its slightly coarse fur. "Guess I'll just have to keep my cute animal friend for myself. How did you end up at the café, anyway? Are you a stray?"

The cat's tail twitched. Maybe she should get a cat toy for it. Wait, when would she get a paycheck? Those were things that she should have considered before—

Part of its white fur moved. As in, moved of its own accord. Lucy stopped scratching behind its ear. Really looked at its pattern as the cat seated itself and looked up at her.

The cat was lanky yet healthy, but the white on its fur was in the shape of a skeleton. Frantically, she checked its back, its tail, and yes, the fur pattern was all the bones of a dog's skeleton!

The white fur shifted again. She realized that it was trying to bark at her.

"Holy—" The girl got to her feet immediately.

At her moving away, the dog skeleton inside the cat seemed to look *sad*. The cat, meanwhile, just looked at her expectantly, apparently missing its pats.

"What is going *on*?" As well as the impression of a white skeleton, there was a small medallion imprinted along the neck. A name in English was written on it in black fur.

Bernie

No way. Her tiny little white terrier?

She'd been walking him with the other dogs when—

"It's not...you, is it?" she asked through very stiff lips.

The cat moved forward, and the dog skeleton looked up at her happily. Lucy got the uncomfortable feeling that it truly *was* happy now that it'd seen her. That was a can of philosophy she didn't want to open today.

Trembling, she could do nothing but stare.

"So he followed you," a man said. Lucy looked up to find that Emil was striding into the room, his red jacket slung over his shoulder. Very inappropriately, he still wore sunglasses.

"What is this?" Lucy asked. He had to have the answers. "And why are you here?"

"I forgot to give you your food card. You can get orange juice and energy bars from the convenience store nearby with it. Some vending machines work, too. There's a limit, though. Don't expect the café to cover anything outside of this."

She had no time to think about how unhelpful that was, seeing as her dog was apparently trapped in the body of a feline. Wordlessly, she took the slim, cream card from him and pointed to the cat with her dog inside of it.

"Affogato," Emil monologued. "One of the most vicious monsters in the café. Did you wonder why a cat would care for someone the moment they stepped inside the building?"

"I...I'm good with animals."

"Affogato would have killed you," Emil said, thoughtful. "He was notoriously hateful. When you died and travelled to this world, you mustn't have come alone. Your pet friend died with you, too."

"Don't...say it like that."

"He arrived here," Emil went on, seemingly uncaringly (he was not pretending; it was a long day), "and loyally waited for you to return. Animals have those kinds of senses, I think, more fine-tuned than monsters. He waited and waited near the spot you were going to arrive at—and then Affogato encountered him and ate him."

Lucy stared at Emil. Her chin trembled.

"My theory is that he was so loyal and his heart so pure that even a monster could not truly destroy him," the man said, looking to Affogato, who was cleaning his paw. "So part of him overtook the cat. His protective nature, and the essence of what he was, stayed and ingrained itself in Affogato. Affected his decisions."

As if understanding this, the cat flicked its tail and neared her for another round of pats. Lucy could barely register its fur under her fingers.

"How could you know?" she asked quietly.

"It's a dog in a cat, Lucy. That's weird even for here. I take notice of things like that. You lived because of him."

Who was now stuck inside a cat that looked mightily annoyed that it wasn't getting more ear scratches.

"That doesn't make any sense," Lucy said, and this time that admission cracked her throat. "None of this makes any sense. I want to go home." She looked in the direction of Tamara's shut door, thought of John. "Let us all go home, Emil, if you can do anything about it."

"I can't do anything about it. Your deaths are final," Emil said. "Nothing can change that or undo what happened in your world. You're stuck here now permanently."

"My world?"

"Yes. People from your world sometimes die and get transported here."

"So this...is this the afterlife?"

"It's simply a different world. Parallel universe, probably."

"What?"

He looked like he wanted to have another smoke, but instead he chose to cut off her questions with, "Sometimes, this world allows for certain souls to teleport here after their death. You and your coworkers have died unfairly. Your livelihoods were taken from you."

"You...know about how I passed?" Wasn't he tuning her out when she told him or something? "Did—Did I get murdered?"

"Perhaps you did, perhaps you didn't. Those whose *livelihoods* have been taken from them appear in this world and work at my establishment. It doesn't mean you're murdered. Your coworkers weren't. It means you were unfortunate to encounter someone who took the possibilities of your life away."

"There were dead people from my past life," Lucy insisted. "Were all of them—?"

"They're a special case. Most of them are the people important to you."

"Amelia's definitely not really important." Petty, but she had to say it. She made care to put as little spite into her voice as she could.

"Important to how you lost your life," Emil added, definitely irritated now. "This is your chance to find out who took your possibilities away. The chance to perform a miracle." He gazed up at the ceiling. "This is a world where those who've wrongly died have the chance to live their life again and find who took their life away."

Lucy toyed with the cuff of her coat. Eventually, she was able to formulate words. "My mum. Is she okay?"

"She's probably still alive in your world."

"How does the café—"

"That's all you need to know." Pointing to her, he added, "Be there before eight tomorrow. I don't want to have to round up my new barista, and I better not find you in a paragraph you're not supposed to be in."

With that, he left, and Lucy stared at the door, her dog trapped inside a cat sitting patiently beside her.

MEANWHILE I

The spirits were gathered out *back* for Pumpkin Soup's funeral. There was no standing room. All were in attendance, from headless Scoville to multi-armed Pepper, who usually couldn't be bothered doing anything much except for playing checkers. Pumpkin Soup had been every spirit's favorite, since he wrought so much destruction. They stood with their heads hung somberly.

Except for Matcha. She kept her head low, but she pushed and weaved through the crowd of spirits to try and find the one she needed to talk to: Habanero.

Normally, she'd have found him beside the monster tied to the fridge. Or he would have been upstairs, passing the time as they usually did when they had no employees to kill nor streets to maim: Playing checkers, burning Ouija boards, participating in target practice, and prank-calling businesses still unfortunate enough to be open in the dead of night.

The mood was bitter. Pumpkin Soup had been all cute and murderous, and a lot of spirits couldn't fathom how a human had managed to defeat him, especially not when he had opposable thumbs. Clearly, it wasn't Habanero's fault; the spirit had slaughtered so many employees that Matcha had lost count. He'd merely been beaten by rotten luck.

She wanted to tell him that she was the new spirit manager. Finally, she had one up on her rival! He'd trained her when she'd appeared in the café, and now it was finally time for the protégée to overtake her mentor.

Couldn't find him in time, though. The procession started. All the spirits stilled as Scoville recited her words for the fallen monster, and the green, stitched-up spirit forced herself to be still.

"You were a good monster, Pumpkin Soup. Every spirit will remember how you hated jokes, had uncontrollable rage, and screamed your opinions. You had the best fashion sense. May you rest in war and bloodshed."

There wasn't much to carry out the funeral rites with, considering that they'd just managed to collect half of a tiny vial of blood. Matcha had forgotten how much damage Affogato could do. Still, Scoville symbolically clutched it.

And then she threw it into the furnace. Flames lit up, rather pathetically, really, like shop-bought fireworks with a fuse that puttered out before it could fire up into the sky. There was barely any heat.

They remained silent for one moment more. Then the spirits broke away, talking, whatever grief they had forgotten. It *was* something other than themselves, after all.

"I don't know what we're going to do with his plaque," one of the older spirits said as Matcha looked around for the one spirit she couldn't seem to find. "It took a ton of spiritual energy to make."

They considered this. Then they unanimously decided that they'd put it by their Ouija- board-for-burning collection. Out of sight, out of mind.

Matcha used her one beaded eye to find Habanero. Finally, in the sea of spirits, she found him!

The spirit with scribbled eyes was walking away, flickering intensely. Wow. Had Pumpkin Soup's death affected him that greatly?

Most likely not, Matcha told herself. Likely, he was still stewing about letting those three imbeciles live.

She went to duck past Pepper and go for him—

"Hold up, Matcha," Scoville said. Her voice was a hiss, considering it was coming out of her mannequin's neck, and it sounded like popping plastic. "We need to talk."

The green spirit turned to find Scoville and three others hanging back. By their faces (or lack of them), she knew something was serious. Scoville did seem to care a bit too much when she was reciting the funeral passage for their dead monster.

Reluctantly, Matcha joined them as the other spirits moved past her and went back up to the second story. "What's this about?"

Scoville looked around. Well, her body turned. It took a bit of interpretation to know what she was doing, but by now Matcha was an expert. "We're concerned about him."

"Why? Because he lost this week?" Matcha did feel the need to defend him, only a little bit, if only because they were definitely rivals that he was definitely aware of.

"No, because..." Pepper trailed off. "...have you noticed that he's a bit upset?"

"I mean, yeah?"

"Matcha." Scoville leaned in. "Habanero was saying that he was a human, once, just a bit after lunch time."

"He left the humans to their own devices," Pepper said, rather disgusted. Her second set of palms began to sweat ink. "And because of that, they won."

"That's stupid. Why would he say that? Habanero would never."

Uncomfortable, Pepper said, "That's what he was muttering about when he thought he was alone. Haven't you noticed that he seems kind of out of it?"

It did seem like the human's lives still being intact was weighing on him. Spirits didn't get sad, they got angry and vengeful.

"I'll ask him," Matcha said.

"No, you can't just ask him!" Pepper yelled.

Didn't matter. Confronting other individuals unnecessarily was a spirit's way. Matcha slipped through the remnants of the crowd and got to the tall, gaunt spirit. "Habanero!"

He turned to her, frowning.

"Are you going around saying that you're a human?" Matcha demanded.

A few spirits gasped.

All at once, he looked outraged. "A human? Who told you that, because I'll rip their eyes out. And if you're making things up, I shall ensure you never speak again *and* rip your one remaining eye out."

He seems *normal.*

Matcha folded her arms over her sewn chest. "Scoville and Pepper were saying that you were prattling on about it. I told them that I didn't believe them, of course." Blaming others and stepping back to watch the carnage was also a spirit's way.

Habanero's scribbled eyes fell on the other two, who strangely weren't there anymore.

"Anyway," Matcha said, gloating. "I've been designated spirit manager this coming week."

At that, Habanero flickered. "...*You'll* be out front from tomorrow?"

"Yes! I'll do what you couldn't and kill them." She threw him a sewn-up smile. Matcha resembled a stuffed bear. Her body consisted of a patchwork of green fabrics tenuously held together by embroidery thread. "I remember what you said, Habanero. Maim them as soon as work starts. Make sure no one comes into the café. Scare the employees witless and make sure that they *can* move for the end of the day!"

Habanero flickered again.

"Afraid that your protégée will kill them before you do?"

"Them? I couldn't care less." Weird. Spirits didn't let go of things so easily. "Only that *I* want the credit!" Okay, that was better.

"I've already decked out the front of the café with all my new traps." Matcha tilted her head. "Actually, I've been meaning to ask you. How *did* the humans get away from you? They look and act like imbeciles."

"They're craftier than they seem," Habanero said.

No speeches? Matcha faltered. These were one-note rebuffs.

"What are they like?" she asked. "The humans."

"One wears far too much leather and is an imbecile. One sleeps all day—but the others quite like possessing her. Keeps them calm."

Silence. It was just them on the lower level, now.

"*...And the barista?*"

Habanero's mouth flatlined. "She's the craftier one," he said. "The craftiest, perhaps. She's very clever." Was he singing her praises?

It didn't sound like he had any vehemence at all. Which was a problem.

"Those are vague, Habanero. How do I kill her? Surely you want her gone."

"Of course I do. I'm simply not telling you how to get rid of her. Why should I help you?" He shrugged his shoulders and vanished far too quickly, leaving Matcha alone.

Now, she was angry, and she busied herself tallying up all the traps she was going to set. Her stitched innards had curdled. Something was up about this new barista. She'd planned rubbing her new role in his face, maybe blackmailing and attempting to torment him, and now what?

She'd tried to find him to celebrate and now she couldn't, all things considered. Something *was* wrong with him. There had almost seemed to be sentimentality in his voice, and that was repulsive. Still, she didn't believe just believe those baseless rumors. Pepper did like causing drama, which was, of course, a spirit's way.

Like a bolt of lightning, a new, radical thought came to her as she listed off the traps she was going to have to set up for the humans. What if...what if they had something on Habanero? What if the humans were wily this time and had managed to blackmail him? That would explain why he let them go so easily and why that random woman seemed to be important somehow.

That was it. Those other two had been slated to die tonight, but it'd all changed when the woman with the beanie arrived. She must have been the reason why. She must have found out a secret of Habanero's.

A human managed to best a spirit!

Unacceptable.

Matcha had humans to manage and kill. And unlike her rival, she wouldn't allow them to live, nor to get one over on her.

Because, she thought in a completely natural and absolutely healthy manner, *I'm the only one who can blackmail Habanero.*

The spirit with scribbles for eyes had three problems.

One, he had a headache. Having all your memories flood back to you in the span of one minute tended to do that to you. Currently, his head felt like it'd been rammed by a heavy human vehicle.

Two, he didn't want to kill a human anymore. He wouldn't give up eliminating all of them, of course. That'd be silly, and he'd be missing out on far too much fun. But his sudden burst of memories told him that the new barista was important to him.

The latte—the latte had made him recall. It'd been in so many memories. Afternoon after afternoon after afternoon, so abundant he'd lost count. And in all those memories, that tall girl with long dark hair and a goofy beanie had been there. He didn't know her name, could only recall bits and pieces of conversations—but he knew she was important and who he had been. Now, when he thought of her...

She reminded him of home.

The third and most glaring problem was that there was a spirit currently taking over whom he'd trained, and because of that, Matcha was definitely going to kill them.

MEANWHILE II

The middle manager of a small shop in the Café Union found himself in the middle of an almost empty room.

The building sat exactly in the center of the city. By this place's standards, it was quite small—ten stories. He'd expected to climb stairs, but instead he'd been led to a room on the first basement floor.

Montgomery, his boss, was the only other person present. At first, he thought he was going to be fired, and he didn't really want Montgomery of all people to say that he was bad at his job (He'd only played online games during his shifts once or twice), but by now he'd realized this was going to be a little different. The middle manager regarded his boss under his lashes and sighed.

"Why is the offer so much money?" the middle manager asked.

The younger man tilted his head. "What do you think is in the middle of the room?"

Practically just thin air. It'd been out of use for months. The manager's dark gaze travelled to the only object in the boarded room: A small, circular table. There was a chain linking its edge to the floor.

The manager wasn't really going to ask, and in all honesty, questions like this, which Montgomery seemed to pose frequently, only served to confuse him.

"It's a table," the man said.

"Are you sure?"

"...Isn't that what a table's supposed to look like?"

"You'd be right, but you'd also be wrong. Look at what happens when you understand it." Montgomery walked forward.

The manager thought that all that unnecessary working out and money had gone to his head and Montgomery had finally lost his wits. He was too afraid to say so, of course. He'd heard through the grapevine that two workers were mortally wounded today, and Montgomery had meted out punishment on the other two for not doing their jobs well enough.

"...Understand the table?" he said instead.

The man didn't look back. "Understand the monster inside the table."

"I don't understand."

Without speaking to him, Montgomery knocked on the edge of the table. Three hollow taps. They echoed through the room, bounced along the walls, and the middle manager thought he'd lost his marbles.

"Sir, I think you should go and have a re—"

Violently, the table shook. Wood twisted open, and out popped something giant on four legs. *It's black as oil—*

That was the only thought the manager could get out before he blinked and found that a monster was right in front of him, snapping and snarling.

He yelled and staggered back, scrambling to get away, but the beast couldn't reach him. It strained against the metal chain that was tethered to the ground, trying to reach him. It looked painful, and the thing looked strong. Hate was in every bite. It even smelled of death.

"This," Montgomery said, "is a monster. Yes, they're real. Emil's café is populated with them. The problem happens when they merge with a piece of furniture. The object becomes cursed, and they can get out of the café that way if someone transports it. If one of these gets angry while outside, it can decimate the populace."

Disbelieving, the middle manager tried to reconcile what he knew about this isle—that it was entirely normal. Sure, they had some work to do on the exploding coffee trade, seeing as the idiot who had invented that was a literal child, but otherwise everything was running normally—with this new information.

"That thing can't exist."

The chain bent.

"But it does," his boss said, rummaging through his expensive pockets. "Most people don't remember them. They've existed here ever since Emil set foot on our ground. Who knows where he and his café came from."

Swallowing, the middle manager stepped away from the monster. People died all the time in this business, of course. That was simple fact. Exploding coffee, café wars from up-and-coming cafés...it was simply the way the coffee business worked. But at least the people they usually went up against were *human*. "Is that why the bonus is so high...?"

"Emil's employees have a coffee cart that's imbued with one of them. We need to get rid of it."

"So you want this part of the Recon team to..." Well, he couldn't quite finish that sentence.

"Retrieve the coffee cart that has a monster a bit like this one inside of it. Disposing of it is obviously best for the people in this city, correct?"

Tongue dry, the manager simply nodded. Inwardly, he thought, *Why not the entire blooming Recon team?*

Montgomery considered this. "We *are* just going to need one of you to retrieve the cart. Wheel it out of there and to our main office, and the money belongs to whomever manages to get it there." He let it sink in.

The bonus was a *lot* of money.

"I mean, what will you do with it once it's here?" the man asked. His eyes tracked the now-familiar horror in disgust.

"Destroy it. It's easier to get rid of something like that in here." Montgomery found what he was looking for and drew something out. A lighter. "You can only kill a monster this far gone if you destroy the piece of furniture or small space it's attached to."

He flicked the flame on. The manager looked to the snarling beast and took in a deep breath.

"Why a quarter of the full Recon team?"

"We're dealing with Emil. Chaos follows him, and the more people that are involved, the worse it gets. With any luck, only a quarter will do."

An awful, niggling feeling pecked at the back of the manager's mind. "Did one of our branches attempt—"

"Something like this a year ago? With the same café in a different location? Yes."

The manager was silent. Now it made sense that, when he'd gone over the books, he'd found that most of the Recon team had quit one year ago. What was Montgomery thinking? Tell the entire branch exactly what they were doing, and they'd walk out.

"This *is* what we have to do," Montgomery added. "It has to do with coffee, so it falls under our jurisdiction."

That thing could cleave through anyone in a second. If he didn't accept the offer and lead the team, he knew that George from HR would be there to overmanage and make it out that the bonus they'd receive was some kind of magic pot of gold with minimal effort required. Unacceptable, really, but...the money would, in all honesty, be worth it.

Teeth flashed white in the darkened room.

"One question," the middle manager finally said. "Do I have to tell them about the monsters? Because I might just leave that part out."

It was simply a series of very monotonous events that led to Lucy Vaudeville ceasing to be.

It'd been sunny, too. That was kind of important.

The twenty-two-year-old started today as she did any other. Shucked on her signature beanie. Threw on her coat, the only decent, good-quality item she owned. She stretched, looked out at the window, made her mother a coffee and left it by her bedside table, kicked on her sneakers, and thought falsely and perhaps far too positively, *Today is going to be a really, really good day.*

Our misguided Lucy had reasons for that. Her confession was rehearsed to the point that she could spout it out line for line at the snap of someone's fingers. Her coffee course was in the morning, making way for walking the dogs in the afternoon. She grabbed her pink backpack and made her way out the door to go to her barista course, her bag brimming with papers.

Outside, Lucy passed the neighbor's cat—ginger, with a perpetually sad look—and gave him a little tummy rub. The last person who had done so had their pinkie torn up. In the distance, she heard trucks thundering on the main street, same as always.

Nothing else of note happened on her walk.

When she got to the barista course's building, though, she took a deep breath in, shook away the last of her sleepiness, and put on her game face. This place was notorious for being a battlefield between her, a few others, and a group of incredibly catty eighteen-to-twenty-year-olds.

A few glanced at her when she entered the double-door threshold. Honestly, she should've been used to it by now. At the very start of her course, it'd been clear that she and Amelia were 'charity cases'; apparently, the course was required to take in a few people with poor secondary academic results with every new initiative. That was partially why this course received funding to give people work placements.

Lucy would probably claw someone's eyes out to get a placement, if she were being honest with herself. Especially if the person whose eyes were being clawed out was Sharon.

Her nemesis in question was currently glaring at Lucy from the row in front of her, eyebrows as sharp as her nails, blonde hair cut severely short, and gloss-covered lips curled into a scowl so terrifying that it was clear she harbored enough hate in her one being to match an entire class's collective souls.

In these four walls, the kitchenette area, and the courtyard at the institute, it was game on.

Lucy decided to continue her three-week-old tradition of giving Sharon the cold shoulder, which she knew would make her even more annoyed. She made a show of sitting down and rustling through her notes, suddenly completely enamored with how cappuccinos were made.

She had plenty of other enemies here, too...

Quinton sat nearby, sandy blond and frowning as she shuffled through her papers. He always did that, though, so she didn't particularly think anything was off that day between her and him. She could simply be breathing and he'd be irritated. Mainly because she'd ticked him off at university, and he knew just how much of an outcast she'd been there.

Then there was Kai. The girl now sitting beside her—when did she get here?—with the long, dark brown hair crammed with bobby pins was *not* her friend, but someone who sometimes dug around for dirt on Lucy, or possibly the answers to their boring, mandatory theory. It was all because Kai wanted to get in Sharon's good books for some reason, and that meant she'd stuck with her ever since Lucy and Amelia's argument. Usually, she annoyed her phone; unfortunately, she was focused on Lucy today. Those contact lenses were boring through her temple, full of unspoken questions that would most definitely get asked when it was the most inconvenient.

Did she hear about me and Sharon's sister?

"Are you ignoring me?" Sharon asked sharply.

"Maybe I am." Lucy didn't look up. Kai took in a sharp, dramatic gasp.

"My sister's not giving you that placement at her café."

As Lucy had found out the day before, when she'd scoped out the café that had promised to take in the aforementioned charity cases if they got a placement.

Long story short: Sharon's sister worked there in upper-middle-management, saw Lucy, and practically bared her pearly white teeth, saying more or less what Sharon was saying now. In much more savage words, Lucy reminded herself, with insults that would put online dictionaries to shame.

"It's not like she owns it," Lucy said.

"Doesn't matter," Sharon volleyed back. "They wouldn't want her to quit. Everyone loves her."

Let's not write fiction. "If I get placed and you don't let me go into work, maybe I'll just have to make a scene for the newspapers," Lucy said brightly.

The two girls next to Sharon suddenly looked unsure.

"You wish you could do that." Sharon turned around in her plastic chair so that her back was to Lucy again, and went on her phone. Was she—?

Great. She was pulling up a group chat with her sister. *Charity Case Hate Club?* Seriously?

Aware of Kai's big eyes focusing on her, Lucy went back to her course notes, trying not to drown in despair and boredom. Although she did catch part of Sharon's following conversation, even though she was adept at tuning her out.

"She was bad at school, and my sister said she was weird. I don't get why now she's suddenly okay at something."

The instructor, who looked more tired than ever, entered the room and waved them into the kitchenette area.

"*Were* you weird in high school?" Kai asked as they began to walk, peering at Lucy as if imagining all of her most embarrassing moments.

"I had more charisma in my fingernails than her sister did in her entire body."

Kai switched over her shoulder.

"Wow, were you listening to Sharon just now? What did you do to her?"

"Huh?"

Kai frowned. "Um, never mind."

And thus an entirely uneventful practical happened. Sharon messed up her hot chocolate and muttered something to Kai at the end. Quinton, bored, made a show of stepping back when it was Lucy's turn to steam her first coffee of the day.

But it didn't faze her. Soon they were back in their class. Kai was on her phone, so Lucy had the chance to focus on what she was going to say to Mikah this afternoon.

"Alright, everyone," the instructor said, clearing his throat. "Thanks for these last three weeks. You all passed, and you're free to go except for five people—the placements. If these people could remain: Quinton, Genevieve, Mateo, Zahara..."

Lucy gripped the table so tightly she thought it might break.

"...and Lucy."

Most people got up to leave, but as they moved, time seemed to stop for Lucy.

A placement.

I got the placement!

"What?" Sharon's protest was muted. Deadly. She strode up to the instructor as everyone left. "No! Lucy can't just get a placement like that. She's practically an old lady."

The instructor's dark eyes rolled upwards. He looked like he just wanted to go to sleep. "I can't do anything about this."

The girl turned on her. "You *can't* have that placement."

Lucy had never heard her so angry.

However...

Good fortune shot to her head, and she didn't handle it well.

"Seethe!" Lucy said, smiling brightly. A perfectly-pointed *f.u.*

Wildly, Sharon looked to the instructor. "You can't be serious!" she shrieked.

"What's done is done," the instructor said. "I can't change your practical, Sharon." Though he looked a little ill saying it. Lucy suspected he would be receiving a complaint from one of the students very soon.

Not that she particularly cared. She had bigger things to worry about, such as confessing to Mikah. So she mentally shrugged it off, waved goodbye to Sharon, skirted Kai, ignored Quinton, whose glare was narrowed, and made her way out of the classroom, thankful it was all over.

*

The park was quiet, though the road around it was terribly busy, with trucks thundering on a wide road just beyond the grass. But that didn't seem to matter, didn't seem quite that important, as she was looking up at Mikah. His hair was blond and curled. His face was broad and handsome. Against the sun, his sea green eyes shone.

What it felt like: She and this boy were the only ones in the park. Even though they were surrounded by women walking their dogs and children screaming at each other on the playground, and some old men were arguing loudly with each other over a chess match, it truly felt like they were alone. With maybe some background ambiance.

In one hand, she held a coffee. Mikah had made it for her. In the other, she held two leashes, one yellow, one red. Bernie yipped, trotting along with Mikah's dog and two others, weaving so that she had to occasionally untangle the leashes. She figured she'd think things over with Bernie and Mikah by her side.

I'm so going to be behind on rent, Lucy thought. Because these two were the only dogs today, and they didn't go very far, she would have to find another job to supplement her part of the rent. Soon. And she wouldn't go and work at a desk. She'd have to find Sharon's sister, prove she was good for that placement, and do so well they could never get rid of her. Maybe she could claw out *her* eyes instead of her sister's...

Here, though, she had some peace of mind, just as long as she was with him.

Mikah had his own dog on a lead. Medium-sized, a golden retriever. She ignored Bernie's yips and followed the smaller three faithfully.

"Okay, so...I've got some news." Lucy looked up at Mikah, searching his face.

The young man smirked at her. "Let me guess. You're moving, and I'll have to up sticks and follow you."

"Nope."

"What, then?"

"I've got a placement."

He whistled. "An actual placement? That means you were in the top five. You've got to tell me which one so I can go there and get my afternoon coffees." He held one in his left hand, the one with glittering rings on all digits.

Lucy pretended to consider it. "It's where my mortal enemy's sister works. She's fighting me over the placement."

"They're just mad that also means you were better than Sharon," Mikah added, laughing easily. "See, Lucy V? I knew you were the best barista there." He nudged her on the arm with his elbow.

"I only know how to make great coffee because you showed me how." Lucy looked down at the paper cup in her hand. He'd made this, too, just before he left work. It felt like home.

With him, everything felt like home.

So she had to confess.

"Okay. So...I really like you, Mikah. Will you go out with me?"

That was about ten sentences shorter than what she'd planned to say to him. She'd spent all that time in the mirror for that? She looked under her lashes at him and decided to roll with her blunder.

Surprise passed on his face—and then he broke out in a grin. "How long?"

"What do you mean, how long?"

"How long have you liked me for?"

"Don't go getting a big ego."

"I like you too, Lucy. Have for some time."

"Some time?"

"Okay, a long while. I just didn't know if you felt the same way." He paused, then shyly said, "Let's see where this goes."

"I'm freaking glad you said yes, because that would have been one awkward dog-walking session." Kind of anticlimactic, but Lucy couldn't help the big grin on her face.

The two of them came to a stop outside the park, next to a road with parked cars. Vehicles slid past. Under the cornflower blue sky, in the cold breeze, Lucy decided to add what she really felt. "I can't imagine a life where you're not in it." That'd been line five of her confession. Couldn't let that one go to waste.

"Honestly? Me neither, Lucy V. It'd be boring without you."

They stood closely together at the crossing.

Today, her life would begin. She felt it in the breeze ruffling through her hair under her beanie, felt it so surely as the buildings on the skyline stood strong. All of a sudden, everything seemed brighter, so much lighter, so much more alive with the promise of something new.

Just for a moment, she savored life.

A horn sounded, incredibly loud, and Mikah's usually placid golden retriever got a fright and barked. At that, she felt a tug on her own leash, looked down—and saw that Bernie had broken free and was darting onto the road.

Without thinking, she shoved the leash for the other dog into Mikah's hands and dashed for her dog.

The traffic was still moving, swerving and honking to avoid him and agitate him by turns. *Just stop driving!* All she remembered was a brief feather of anger. Behind her, Mikah's dog and the other two had whipped into a frenzy.

A car nearly clipped her elbow. She shrieked but still went for Bernie, who was now cowering, whimpering.

"Lucy!" yelled Mikah.

In the din, he might have run up to her. Maybe. She felt that he did, but hoped that he wouldn't.

Something seemed to bend the air.

The metal grating of a vehicle hit her at full force. An impact, the quick, heavy force of pain.

Then everything went black.

*

An alarm blared from the bedside table, and she opened her eyes to find her plain white pillow stained with tears.

Not bright and sunny but dark, with stuffy, filtered neon shining through the curtains. Despite the intense color, it looked so gentle. Lucy thought about that briefly, feeling not much at all for a moment, taking in small breaths. She wiped at her tears. Her hand was sore...

She was aware of a presence near her, and she remembered where she was, and all the dreams of yesterday and her life before evaporated here in this strange world.

At the foot of her bed was Affogato—and what was left of Bernie. The cat slept soundly. Couldn't really believe what it was capable of. *A cat can never normally kill a dog. Is this the world's way of balancing those kinds of things out?*

Affogato's eyes weren't open. She felt something else watching her.

The presence nearby was, she found, Emil. The door was open. His sunglasses were, of course, still on.

The man leaned against the doorframe. How long had he been glaring at her like that for?

"Are you finished?" he asked, tone curt.

"Are you serious?" she muttered. It was the first thing out of her mouth. "Why are you *here*?"

"Shop's about to open."

Outside was night.

"We've got an intense day ahead of us at the café," Emil said.

"...Okay. Get out so I can have a shower."

Affogato opened one green eye, seemingly watching Emil. The man shrugged, strode away, and called, "Don't be late. Oh." He

117

reappeared just before the door could close and tossed something through the gap. It landed on the floor unceremoniously. "Here's a reward."

A paycheck?

Not quite.

"…Huh. You even have Crocs here, too."

*

Lucy left the apartment snacking on an apple with Affogato by her side. The cat…monster…really was like a dog, switching by her side, sitting patiently in the elevator, and keeping as close to her as it could. People actually made way for it. She got a couple of elbows, though.

Those signs with cats on them seemed to stare at her. They were illuminated with neon lighting, making the shadows cast on them look crescent-shaped. Still swamped in darkness, the city breathed, the heights sparkling above her as lights flicked on one by one from top to bottom and the scent of hot food began to waft from various shops.

She got to the entrance of the café and found John standing outside, his arms folded. The leather and ripped trousers didn't seem to do much to keep out the cold; he was shivering, and his face looked paler and more ill. *Wouldn't put on a uniform like the rest of us, huh.*

Tamara stood beside him. Must've slipped outside of the apartment complex without telling Lucy. Her gaze was on the awnings, though she saw Affogato, and a cloud of doubt covered her face.

John gave a short nod. "Thank you for yesterday," he said.

Lucy's heart warmed as she turned her attention back to them. "I…don't save lives often." Her breath frosted.

Tamara tucked a strand of loose pink hair behind her pointed ear. "Are we going to do this?"

"How do we get out of here?" Lucy asked, feeling the tension of the fabric of her bandaged hand. "Is there even the possibility of a way out of here? Also, where did you go last night, John?"

John looked out at the silent city, at the pedestrians still strolling along the sidewalks. His rugged face was pensive.

"…I'm working on something." He flexed his tanned fingers thoughtfully. "We'll try the key today. There's a loophole in what we agreed to do. There's got to be."

Tension washed over them as cars sleepily slid by on the road behind Lucy.

Emil seemed to think that they were about to open, but they had plenty of time. No one made a move to go into the café. Lucy looked between the two of them and couldn't help it.

118

"Why did you end up here?" she asked. At John's raised brows and Tamara's sideways glance, she jolted and said, "I was just told why I was here. Emil said yesterday that the reason we're at this café is to...make things right." The final words sounded too childish, too simple, but she couldn't find any other way to say it. "Not trying to be rude or anything. I just, well, wanted to know if you were in the same boat."

"I'm not sure why Tamara is here," John said. "But my reason's b.s."

That's...entirely unhelpful, Lucy thought.

"Do we really want to recount how our opportunities were taken from us?" Tamara added, seeing her expression.

At that, Lucy couldn't really argue.

"Anyway. We can't stay out here forever." John nodded to the darkened windows of Café Teras. "We'd hoped you'd show up today." He held up the key. "You ready to get out of here?"

And leave Emil behind in the dust? "Heck yeah."

Together, the three of them were determined. But despite their words, they didn't enter the café right away. If anything, they wanted to stay under the awning for just a little bit longer, the only people from Earth in a city somewhere far away from home...

Afterword

Thank you so much for reading!

Lucy's story is far from over. There will be six novellas in total that make up *A Coffee Somewhere Between Dangerous and Boring*.

Travelling to another city brought on the idea for this series. Every town has its own personality. A city with busy roads and skyscraper is distinct from the tiny country town right next to it not just by its landmarks but by its way of life and its feel. What would it be like to visit a city that isn't for people to stay in? That has its own personality that you'd have to stay in for years to understand? That thought and the first impression of stepping somewhere new was the beginning of what inspired me to put what conjured a feeling of being out-of-place onto paper.

After putting the first arc online (late 2024!), it underwent some heavy editing. Thanks to some sleepless nights, too many cups of black tea, and an overworked laptop, the first arc is in its final rendition!

One word about the digital version: The series in its digital form will always be free. I will never charge for the electronic version on any of the books in this series.

Speaking of which, you can find the web serial's updates on its official site: https://acoffeesomewherebetween.wordpress.com/

Character Sketches